# MORT THE MEEK

### AND THE
### PERILOUS
### PROPHECY

## RACHEL DELAHAYE

## ILLUSTRATED BY GEORGE ERMOS

# LITTLE TIGER

## LONDON

# TO READ THIS STORY, YOU NEED TO VISIT BRUTALIA

But Brutalia doesn't like visitors, so don't approach
anyone, and keep your eyes peeled for escape
routes, and remember to creep and scuttle to avoid
being seen, and wear brown so you blend in.
Look, it's probably best if you just
disguise yourself as a **RAT.**
OK with that?
If you are, then step this way.
Step this way, but watch out for traps...

# CHAPTER ONE
# A FIGHT WITH A FUNNY TASTE

*"Have you heard the word?
There's a revolution!"*

*"That's just a rumour going
round and round."*

The town square was a riot. It was as if the entire population of Brutalia had been put into a tumble dryer – except instead of making people dry, it was making them angry. Folk were flying through the air, tearing out each other's hair and pinching everywhere, and the island echoed with insults, shouts and screams. A totally ordinary day in Brutalia, then... Only, this time two boys were worried that *they* had somehow started the fight.

Big deal! Fights have to be started by someone, right?

Ah, but these two boys were pacifists. They didn't believe fighting was the answer to anything – not even the question, **What rhymes with lighting and starts with f?** That's just how against it they were. So, if they *had* somehow kicked off the violent brawl, then ... AWKWARD.

Mort Canal, plumber's son and founder of the Pacifist Society of Brutalia, dodged a well-aimed pumpkin and stared despairingly at the devastation around them. Next to him, his best friend, Weed Millet, the baker's son, was squealing like a squeezed chicken.

"Surely this can't be because of us," he squawked. "Our whole message was about extending the hand of kindness."

"I know," Mort yelped, ducking a speeding potato. "And everyone's extending fists of ferocity!"

They scurried behind a barrel as three old ladies barrelled past, tangled up like a ball of rats. Old ladies were often the worst. They lived longer than the average Brutalian, so had more experience and lots of time to form really deep-seated grudges.

"What on earth's going on?" Weed cried.

Mort caught a small girl who had been catapulted over his head. "There you go, little one," he said, placing her safely on solid ground.

She kicked him in the shin and ran off to rejoin the fight. Then she came back and bopped him on the nose.

"Pacifist!" she shouted with glee and scarpered. Then she came back again and stamped on his foot.

"OW! Did you hear that, Weed? She said *pacifist*! It **is** because of us. We need to find out how this happened!"

Weed tugged at Mort's tunic. "I don't think there's time. Lance Pollip is staring at you funny!"

Lance Pollip was the 'boil doctor' of Brutalia. **Pollip's Pop-Shop** was guaranteed to burst your boils, prick your pimples and puncture your pustules, but common side effects of treatment included redness around the affected area and totally avoidable death.

"Mort the Meek!" Lance bellowed, lumbering towards them, his alarmingly large thumbs wriggling.

The present members of the Pacifist Society of Brutalia gulped.

While Mort and Weed are busy gulping, let's have a chat about Brutalia's strange affection for fighting. You may already know about it, but if you don't then steady your guts and hold your loved ones close, because pain and distress can be painful and distressing. And in Brutalia fighting came with a side of super-strength OUCH. Anyone thinking they could pop down the vegetable market and return without a scratch must have been born yesterday. Or born somewhere nice. And there was nothing nice about Brutalia. If you need convincing, then just take a look at its traditional nursery rhymes:

*'Twinkle Twinkle Battle Scar'*

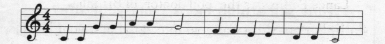

*'If You Go Down to the Woods Today,
You're Sure to be Ambushed'*

*'Bumpty Thumpty Sat on a Spike'*

As you can see, a good dust-up in the square was as normal and inevitable as a jam sandwich.

But there WAS something different about this particular scuffle. It had a strange taste to it, like a jam sandwich with a thin spread of tuna. And it had all kicked off when the Pacifist Society of Brutalia handed out their promotional leaflets.

Mort and Weed had been trying to encourage people to turn to peace, so what was it about these words that had made them turn on each other instead? What had unleashed such mayhem?

But quickly! Let's race like rats and catch up with the boys before we find ourselves squished between the giant thumbs of Lance Pollip or ambushed by kids singing happy little songs of destruction...

**"RING-A-RING-A-ROSES,**
**WEDGE A HEDGEHOG UP YOUR NOSES!"**

Mort and Weed wove through the crowd, trying to

get away from Lance Pollip. But it's hard to weave when there are no spaces to weave into, and the pimple-popper was closing in on them. Suddenly a space opened up, and they rushed towards it, tasting freedom ... before an old lady tripped up Mort with a very large parsnip, and he landed flat on his back. Lance Pollip loomed above him, and it looked as if it was all over.

## PA-PA-PA-PA PER-PA PIDDLY PA!

Saved by the parp! At the sound of the royal horn, everyone put down their victims and vegetables and turned to face the stage – a raised wooden platform where people were punished or pickled, all for the Queen's entertainment. Oh yes, the ruler of Brutalia was a nasty piece of work. She spent her days guzzling oysters and kicking her King for spending his days guzzling oysters, which made her a right old hypocrite. Her favourite things were fashion crimes and punishment. The first was revolting, and the second was absolutely terrifying.

It looked as if the Queen was pretty pleased with whatever she had in store because she had brought her entourage. As well as all her guards, there were Grot Bears* and Grot Bear handlers.

After the Grot Bears came the King, who was wheeled out only on special occasions (and by wheeled we mean carried on his sofa on the backs of four small children). And then there was silence. The crowd searched the King's face for a clue as to what was about to happen – but he didn't have a periwinkle's inkling, and he stared ahead blankly like a boiled potato until his Queen arrived, which she did to the insufferable accompaniment of more parping horns.

She was wearing a gown made of sad squirrels and was astride her least favourite manky-breath tiger, Warren. Warren was being led by the Queen's new personal bodyguard, Marcus Sucram, who was

*What's a Grot?
Grot Bear is short for Grotesque Bear – a species of enormous mammal with a stubborn head, a slab of a tongue and razor claws. They come in two subspecies – the Grot Bear that *hates* everything it sees and rips things apart, and the Grot Bear that *loves* everything. (It's about the only affection you'll find on Brutalia, but it's short-lived because the loving Grot Bear hugs whatever it loves to absolute death in seconds.)

chosen purely because his name was spelled the same backwards.

Thanks to the arrival of the hideous royals, Lance Pollip left Mort alone. But it didn't mean the pressure was off, because the Queen arriving at the beginning of the story could only mean one thing: something big was about to happen. And, as nothing nice ever happened in Brutalia, it was bound to be deeply unpleasant.

# CHAPTER TWO
# SOUP, FOR STARTERS

*"Have you ever had been
accused of anything?"*

*"I've been accused of being a
looker, which is nice."*

*"You do have a habit of staring
at people, Ratty."*

The guards raised their *CLAP NOW* and *CHEER NOW* signs, which prompted the crowd to clap and cheer. Although the Queen was full of hate, she did like to be adored. And, for anyone thinking of *not* adoring her, the punishment was clear – and MURKY – because the details were written on the chalkboard for all to see.

## PUNISHMENT
### OF THE DAY

You will be plunged
into a hot bog.

By hot, I mean boiling, and by
plunged, I mean held under.

By bog, I mean a swamp
with added ingredients.

By added ingredients,
I mean ... WAIT AND SEE.

What added ingredients? Piranhas? Old bananas? You can't be prepared for what you don't know. Therefore, while some Brutalians might have happily endured a bog bath for hygiene reasons (because nothing could make them filthier), not a single soul wanted to **WAIT AND SEE**.

People are sometimes more afraid of what they don't know than what they do know. Did you know that? Now you do know, so keep it in mind because, you know, it'll help you understand what this story is all about (if it ever gets going).

# GET ON WITH IT!

All right, all right, keep your pants on...

So the citizens of Brutalia continued their adoring applause with sore hands and raw throats until finally the Queen motioned to the guards to lower their signs.

**"MY LOYAL SUBJECTS!"** she shouted. "I have gathered you all here today because I want to test your knowledge."

She said it with suspicious delight, and the crowd's brains itched in panic because knowledge wasn't one of their strongest subjects.

"First question – if I told you to clap, what would you do?"

She stared accusingly at the wall of silent faces in front of her. "You **CLAP**, you idiotic mushrooms! You *CLAP*!"

Someone stupidly clapped, and the Queen's face purpled. "Not **NOW**, you absolute flannel! Next question – what's Brutalia's main sporting event?"

There were murmurs of confusion in the crowd because this seemed to be some kind of painless quiz. Eventually, a bold character shouted, **"The Annual Cabbage Drag!"**

The Queen nodded approvingly. "Question three – what do we do with the losers of the Annual Cabbage Drag?"

Emboldened by the previous shouter coming to no harm, Brutalia's only comedian, Looby Larkspit, called out, "Make them fart 'God Save the Queen'?"

There was a tight silence, but the Queen let it go. So did the King, and thirteen people fainted.

"And the final general-knowledge question," the

13

Queen said, holding her nose. "Does Brutalia **like** visitors or does it **hate** visitors?"

This was an easy one.

**"BRUTALIA HATES VISITORS!"** everyone shouted gleefully, hoping there might be a prize.

The Queen smiled and batted her eyelids, which were adorned with millipedes for a full-volume lash effect. "Excellent response. And now on to today's *businessssssssssssss*."

The Queen stretched out her s's, which annoyed everyone, but especially Warren the tiger, who roared. His manky breath poisoned the air, and the crowd cowered. It looked like the Fun Quiz was over.

"Snit Parlot has overheard something **VERY DISTURBING**."

---

**A SMALL NOTE FOR EAGLE-EYED READERS**
If you're a keen reader of Mort, you'll remember that once upon a time the Queen welcomed a bunch of foreign poshos in the hopes of finding a new King. Well done you for spotting that. But, if you think about it, they weren't visitors... They were VICTIMS. Would YOU like to be married to the Queen? Exactly! (See how writers are tricky – they always make up things!)

*GASP NOW* signs went up, and everyone gasped very easily. For what could a Queen who was wearing sad squirrels and wriggling eyelashes possibly find disturbing?

"*What could it be?*" Weed whispered.

"I dread to think," Mort said. His stomach had dropped the moment she said the name Snit Parlot. The Royal Snoop was always getting the wrong end of the stick, and it always had a sticky ending.

"And who did he overhear, you ask?"

The Queen beady-eyed the crowd. And the crowd beady-eyed each other suspiciously until there was a loud:

# CRUNCH!

(it looked like it was crunch time)

## "SALLY McROOT!" the Queen shrieked.

The guards lifted their signs and the crowd went, '*OOH.*'

"I ain't done *nothing*!" came a frail voice from somewhere in the throng.

"*She hasn't done anything,*" Weed whispered to Mort.

"Grammatically correct," Mort agreed. "She's just a soup maker and bum-shaped vegetable enthusiast."

They watched, terrified, as Sally was tossed like a rugby ball through the crowd and across the square to the front. Guards lifted her on to the stage, and she trembled before the Queen, who beckoned to Snit Parlot. The Royal Snoop slid towards her like a well-oiled trolley, licking his well-oiled lips.

"This is the old woman you overheard?"

"It certainly is, Your Majesty," Snit oozed.

"Can you recount the events of that afternoon for us all?"

"Indeed I can, Your Majesty," he syruped.

"Well, do it, then!"

"Absolutely, certainly, you betcha, Your Highness." Snit cleared his throat. "I was passing Sally McRoot's house when I saw smoke at her window. The sort of smoke you would expect from a sorcerer's magic potion."

16

Guards help up their **OOH NOW** signs.

## *Ooooooooh!*

"It was steam!" Sally spat. "Steam from my soup pot."

"It smelled unsavoury," Snit said. He circled the old woman, taunting her with his slippery confidence.

"My soups *always* smell unsavoury," Sally grumbled.

"But the steam smelled *evil*," Snit insisted.

"That's going too far. I do my best with what I've got. I'd give my nostrils for an ingredient that didn't taste of mud and mould."

"I listened at the window..."

Mort sighed. What perfectly innocent words had Snit Parlot got tangled up this time?

"...and I heard her say: '*When it's bubbling, I'll see in my head.*'"

## "WHAT DOES IT MEAN?"

the Queen shouted. Her tiny hazel-gazey eyes glistened as if she already knew the answer. She rubbed her hands together with glee.

17

"*When it's bubbling, I'll see in my head* means ... Sally McRoot can read her soup!" said Snit.

"Aha!" the Queen screeched. "A soup sayer!"

"Rubbish!" Sally shouted. "I ain't a soup sayer! I don't even know what a soup sayer is."

"*What is a soup sayer?*" Weed whispered.

"No idea," Mort admitted.

"A soup sayer is someone who tells the future in their soup!" the Queen clarified. "And it looks like you've been reading your soup without a soup-reading licence."

"I have not!" Sally spat. "I just said that when the soup's bubbling I'll see to my bread. I dip it in my soup. It's nothing new, y'know."

"That's not what I heard," Snit Parlot sang tauntingly.

The Queen dismounted Warren and put the tip of her long finger on Sally's nose, wiggling it as she spoke. "We know the punishment for future-telling without permission, don't we?"

"DEATH!" shouted some particularly nasty sorts in the crowd. "DEATH! DEATH! DEATH!"

"Unfortunately, we don't do that here any more," the Queen said, and her own nose wrinkled like an overboiled sausage, and her lips puckered like a rat's bottom.

*"No executions any more! That's thanks to you in Book One, that is,"* Weed whispered, nudging Mort.

The Queen momentarily glazed over as she remembered the good old days, and the King put a caring arm of condolence round her shoulders and whispered, *"There, there, my prickly pear."*

She shrugged off her husband and his drivelling pity.

"Execution may be against the law ... **BUT** – and it's a **BIG BUT** – Snit Parlot overheard something else, didn't you, Parlot?"

"Indeed I did, Your Majesty," he slimed. "I heard her say, *'Fiends are scheming.'*"

**"FIENDS!"** the Queen shrieked, making it sound very scary indeed.

Even without *PANIC NOW* signs, people began to panic and it boiled over into a mass fight, the likes of which no one had seen since just a bit earlier.

"SO," the Queen said, "when it comes to Sally

McRoot's punishment, I am forced to make an exception."

Weed looked at Mort, horrified. "She can't bring back execution, can she?"

Mort swallowed a lump the size of a toad as he looked up at poor Sally, who was quaking like windy lettuce.

"But I—" Sally McRoot tried to protest, but she was prodded by Marcus Sucram. "Ow!"

The Queen continued. "She will be given an exec—"

"But—" Sally was poked again. "Stop it!"

"She will be given an executive new kitchen and vegetables with no mouldy bits so that she may keep Brutalia safe with her soupy predictions," the Queen said. "From now on, she will be known as the Royal Soup Sayer."

The Queen turned to Sally, who was now blinking rapidly like a lizard with an eye infection.

"What is it you wanted to say, Sally McRoot? Spit it out."

Sally McRoot was about to inform everyone that she had only uttered the words, "*The beans are steaming.*" But now she wasn't headed for death or prison, she decided to keep her mouth shut about that.

"I just wanted to say *the fiends are scheming* again," she said, with a little smile. "Oh yes, they're schemey-scheme-scheming. Soup says so."

The Queen stamped her foot and pointed her bony finger at the crowd. "Everyone must be alert. The strangers may already be on our shores. And we don't like strangers on Brutalia, let alone strangers that are fiendish. Throt Gutsem!"

A man stepped forward. He was tall, with biceps as big as baby cows and eyes the colour of steel. His cropped hair was thick and tufty like a doormat, and his expression was so fiercely intense, it would scare the skin off a rat. Even a pretend rat.

Throt Gutsem was Brutalia's brutal Battle-Chief, and his presence made one thing clear – the Queen was serious. And, although the execution of a Brutalian citizen was no longer allowed, there was nothing in the documents that said you couldn't kill strangers.

He beat his breastplate with his fist. "At your service, Your Majesty. No one invades my homeland and lives to tell the tale!"

You'd have to pity any strangers who decided to visit Brutalia, wouldn't you?

But don't worry. No one ever did.

# CHAPTER THREE
# TWO FACES AT CRASHBANG COVE

*"Oi, Ratto, what's a toucan?"*

*"One more than a one-can."*

*"Heh-heh-heh."*

Fear fell over Brutalia like an itchy blanket. Where were these troublemakers? What did they look like? What would they do?

But such troubling questions were quickly forgotten when Mort and Weed's leaflets, which had been stirred up by the sneeze of a Grot Bear, fluttered back down to the ground. The landlord, Publinka Dunker, kicked off the fighting by throwing a barrel at Stubber Peckitall, the pigeon-keeper, and, as three old ladies rolled past, Mort shook his head sadly.

"I don't believe it!" he sighed. "It's happening again!"

"And you won't believe this, Mort ... but Lance Pollip is still looking at you funny."

"Run, Weed. *RUN!*"

The two boys shot, fast as rats down the broken backstreets and sickly side streets of Brutalia. Round every corner, people were brawling and, above them, their leaflets swirled on the breeze like symbols of hope before landing in pools of plop.

"I don't know how much more of this I can take," Weed panted. "What's the point in spreading kindness if it just makes people angry?"

They heard a roar of, **"MORT THE MEEK!
I WANT A WORD WITH YOU!"** – Lance Pollip
was close – and Mort pulled Weed into a teeny-tiny
passageway. They held in their conversation and
sucked in their bellies as they edged through the
narrow gap to the other end, where they let it all out
again.

"Fighting for what's right without fighting is always
a bit of a struggle," Mort said. "But, if we surrender, the
war on violence will be over."

He realized he'd used quite a lot of aggressive words
for a pacifist and shuffled awkwardly.

"You're just upset, that's all," Weed said, spotting
his discomfort. "Why don't we recite the Pacifist
Promise?"

"Good idea, Weed."

They breathed in deeply, placed their hands on their
hearts, and flared their nostrils because it felt like a
passionate thing to do. Then they said the words:

*"I, a member of the Pacifist Society of
Brutalia, promise not to hurt anything."*

They unflared their nostrils and felt a lot better about everything. With their hope topped up and Lance Pollip stuck at the other end of a very narrow passage, they took a moment to look around.

The teeny alley had brought them to clifftops on the west side of the island, overlooking Crashbang Cove. It was a most perilous bight (a curved nibble out of the land), which also looked like a bite (a curved nibble out of a biscuit), where the waves slapped against razor-sharp rocks and the water hissed with danger. Down in the puking swash, a boat was being tossed about, and there were two people on board.

"What are they doing?" Weed gasped.

"Everyone knows Crashbang Cove is a death trap, so my guess is that they're not from around here."

"You mean they're ... STRANGERS?"

"I don't know. It would be extremely strange if strangers came to our strange island acting all strange just after we've had a chapter about the dangers of strangers."

Weed widened his large chocolatey eyes. "*The Soup Prophecy...*"

"I don't believe for a moment the soup said anything at all," Mort said. "And if our future really does depend on soup then we're doomed."

The air slurped with the promise of interesting plot, and it rang with an eerie, echoey clang.

## DING-A-LING! DING-A-LING!

"Is that a Clanging Chime of Doom?" Weed said, with a wobbling chin.

"No, I think that's Punky ringing the lookout bell."

"Good old Punky," Weed said, with a smile.

Punky Mason was the newest member of the Pacifist Society of Brutalia. She was once a rock-crusher with a terrible voice, and now she was an animal-lover with a terrible voice. But that sort of thing is a matter of opinion because, although Mort and Weed thought her singing sounded like a dinosaur throwing up a combine harvester, there were kids who were in awe of it. In fact, some had even stopped kicking shins and instead thrashed out all their anger at her rock concerts.

Another lover of her voice was the Belgo, a giant three-armed sea monster, and Punky's job was to look out for him in Brutalia's waters. This was to protect the fishing boats. The Belgo was fond of juggling them.

Mort and Weed thought lovingly of their fellow pacifist as they looked down into the swell. Which wasn't swell – it was absolutely awful.

"If the Belgo gets hold of that little boat, they'll be lucky to live another day," Weed said.

"And, even if the Belgo doesn't get them, they're dangerously close to the rocks."

"They'll be thrown overboard! They'll perish! They'll be eaten by ravens!"

"And then we'll never find out what this CHAPTER is all about. Let's rescue them."

"But they could be fiends!"

"They could also NOT be fiends, Weed. Either way, we cannot stand by and let them die."

There was a cackling from above. A swarm of ravenous ravens, clacking their beaks at the thought of fresh guts and brains, circled the clifftop scene.

In the shadow of their dark cloaks, Mort and Weed descended the dizzying cliffs. The wind whistled round their ears, and cliff rats nibbled their knees, and, when their feet finally touched the rocks below, things didn't get much better. Half submerged in the ice-cold sea, the angry wash crashed against them, soaking their clothes and stinging their scratched shins with its high salt content.

"I hope we get a thank you from the strangers after all this," Weed said. He flicked a carnivorous clam from his earlobe.

Mort was struggling – gently, of course – with a strong-willed squid, which had wrapped its arms round his neck. "Let's worry about that after we get everyone to safety."

Holding on to each other, they searched the bubbling waters. But there wasn't a single stranger, and where the boat had been playing Buckaroo there were now just a few sodden planks floating on the foam. One had neat writing – swirly and fancy but not illegible, which was sensible.

"Oh no," Mort sobbed. "Those poor people. Whoever they were."

"Now they're on the seabed being munched by carnivorous clams," Weed added.

"Yes, best not to think about that."

"Sucked by fat-lipped sea cucumbers."

"Stop it, Weed."

"Skinned by giant flesh-eating wimps."

"I think you mean shrimps. Now, listen," Mort said sternly. "It will do our sore hearts no good to think about what grisly things might be happening to them now. Instead, let's feel sad a while. We don't know who they are or where they came from, but we do know that there are two faces that will now never be seen again."

# "YOOOHOOOO!"

Mort and Weed looked up. At the top of the cliff, two faces were looking down at them.

"Are those the two faces we were just talking about, Mort?"

## A COUPLE OF HOURS LATER...

Mort and Weed heaved themselves back up the cliff, and there at the top were the strangers with two faces (one each, that is). They were two girls – one with short, curly ginger hair and the other with cascading wavy brown locks.

The rose glow of the setting sun highlighted their fine cheekbones and strong noses, and they stood so still and straight they looked like statues. Or certainly like people who were aware of their posture. Their immaculate white robes fluttered in the breeze, and, from a distance, they didn't seem evil, but the large bird at their feet was a bit unnerving. It was

black and white, with a rainbow beak so luminous, it
must have been poisonous.

"Wh-wh-who are you and what do you want?"
Weed shouted.

The red-haired one spoke. "I'm Vita and
this is Genia, from the tropical island of
Bonrock. I say, do you have some kind
of sweating disease?"

"We're sweating because we just
climbed a cliff," Mort said.

"Although neither of you look
very ... moist."

"That's because we're
extremely fit," Vita said.

"And clever," added
Genia, flicking her hair.

Mort and Weed gulped.

"We found an easier route up just a bit further along," she continued. "Took fifteen minutes, tops. We tried to whistle but you didn't hear us."

"Are you dangerous?" Weed asked.

"Well, we've got fierce intellects..." Vita said.

The girls tipped their heads back and laughed. It was a laugh that tinkled like the high notes on a piano, and it made Mort and Weed feel really quite giddy. The enchanting spell was broken when their strange bird started croaking like a frog.

"What *is* that?" Mort said, leaping back. "Is it venomous?"

"Not at all. It's my toucan," Genia said. "We lost Vita's down there somewhere. It'll find its way home."

"I don't—" Weed began.

Mort pulled Weed to one side. "It's probably best if we don't go through all the ways their bird could have died in the Salty Sea. It might upset them. And we don't want to upset them."

"Why?" Weed's eyebrows trampolined up and down. "Do you think they're fiends?"

"Honestly, I don't know. We don't know what

we don't know."

"How do you know?"

"You *don't* until you know."

At that moment, chanting drifted from the town.
Voices shouting as one.

# "KILL THEM STRANGERS!"

"Kill THOSE strangers," Genia tutted.

Mort and Weed looked at each other nervously.
Clever and strange... If they didn't hide these girls
quickly, they wouldn't stand a chance. And everyone
deserves a chance.

# CHAPTER FOUR
# ONCE WRITTEN, TWICE SHY

*"These strangers are not like us, Ratty."*

*"In what way are they not like us, Ratto?"*

*"They've had a bath!"*

Back in the town, Sally McRoot had been stirring.

For a reclusive soup maker and bum-shaped vegetable enthusiast, it turned out she quite liked the attention. Being flavour of the month was exciting, and her new role as Royal Soup Sayer was really rather tasty. You couldn't blame her. She had been given access to vegetables with no mould and a fantastically big cauldron. And, to keep the supply of free vegetables coming, she had been concocting **MANY** portions of predictions.

They'll nick your lunch

You'd be better off dead

Everything you know will be gone

Fiends are scheming

They'll steal your kids

Sally's predictions ran round the town like rats on a hot tin roof, sending everyone into a frenzy. There were fights (of course) and vandalism (of course) and a new phenomenon: graffiti. This happens when people feel things so strongly that they want to shout. But shouting evaporates too quickly, so they paint their shouts on to anything that paint sticks to, to make them last longer.

As Mort led the others into the town, this is what they saw, scrawled in vicious writing along the sides of houses, on walls, on rodents with hot feet, on absolutely everything:

STRANGERS
ARE DANGERS

KILL
THE
SKEEMERS

wotch out for peepol wot do not live here

I hate soup

BEWARE!
Fiendish strangers are
a-coming...

Vizzy-tors are boils
on the bottom of
Brutalia

Kevin smells of rat poo

If Genia and Vita wanted to discuss the spelling deficiency of Brutalia, they clearly decided not to. Because frightening words spelled wrong are still frightening.

Weed picked up a loaf of bread that was lying in the gutter. Bread made by his very own family business. Words had been written on the top of it in chocolate. But this is Brutalia, so it probably wasn't chocolate...

"It says **Keep Strangers Out**. Oh dear... It looks like my parents are also involved. We can't go back to mine."

"We'll have to go to my house," Mort said. "Here, put these on."

He handed the strangers some tatty rat-coloured rags to cover their white robes, and they snuck through the slippery side streets and brawling backstreets of Brutalia. Beneath their hoods, Vita and Genia's eyes were wide like boiled eggs as they saw filth in every nook and fights in every cranny. They heard wails and cries and noises best not investigated, and above them ravens circled like a dark fog, their scissor beaks snapping.

When they reached Mort's house, Kennet Canal was out fixing a sewer and Avon was round at the neighbours' having a ding-dong with a full dinner set. Only his sister and brother – Gosh and Gee – were there, sitting at the kitchen table, giggling like squids and counting their knocked-out teeth.

Mort ushered Vita, Genia and Weed into the next room, while he sorted them out.

"Hi, Mort. I got Gee's incisor, two of his canines and a big fat molar," Gosh whistled delightedly through her gappy grin.

"I got four of Goth's – thoo from the front and thoo from the back," Gee lisped.

Mort twisted their teeth back into their gaping gum holes with a paste of marigold pulp while the twins gargled threats to knock them back out again.

Gosh and Gee loved each other to bits (and pieces), but they were Brutalian through and through. They had their own sibling games of Bash-up-before-bedtime and Bash-up-before-breakfast, and they often pestered their big brother to join in. Mort always refused. That's how he got his nickname **Mort the Meek,** which stuck like a fly on a sticky bun (just don't ask why the bun was sticky).

"There you go," he said, pushing the last tooth into its pit. "Before you go out again, tell me what started the fight this morning. What did it say on the leaflets that made everyone want to punch each other's noses?"

Gosh shrugged. "I dunno. I can't read, can I?"

Since the only reading teacher, Leggo Mentis, lost a lethal game of tiddlywinks, there was no one to teach the little'uns how to read. Of course, Mort had tried to tutor Gosh and Gee, but every time he opened his mouth the little crabsticks wanted to make his teeth wobbly. So he'd given up on that.

When his siblings were out of the way, Mort made tea with hot water and dried grass, and half the Pacifist Society of Brutalia and two Might-be-Enemies then sat round the table, looking at each other funny. Not funny ha-ha but funny *peculiar*. Mort and Weed were nervous because they were harbouring illegal strangers, and Vita and Genia were nervous because, well, you would be if you'd seen the writing on the walls and the filth on the floor. It was both unfriendly and unhygienic.

"Why is everyone writing and shouting bad things about strangers?" Vita asked.

"The Queen's Soup Sayer said she saw suspicious, scheming strangers in her soup."

"That's a lot of s's," Genia giggled. "You know you don't have to be scared of us, don't you?"

Mort didn't know because he didn't know what he didn't know. But maybe he'd relax if he knew a little bit more. To know more you have to ask questions.

"Why are you here?"

"We're doing a project on Brutalia. No one has ever dared to come to this place before, and we thought we'd get top marks if we did. Genia likes to get top marks," Vita said.

"Top marks from who?" Weed asked.

"From whom," Genia corrected.

Vita elbowed her. "Don't be rude!" She turned to Mort. "Our teacher, of course. Do you know what teachers are?"

Mort gulped. "Yes, I had one once. Leggo Mentis. He taught me to read."

"We need to remember that for the project, Genia.

Brutalians can read."

"Not all of them," Mort said hurriedly, not wanting to give them false information. "As it happens, we're quite confused. Our leaflet just caused absolute chaos, and we don't know why. Maybe you can help."

He pushed one across the table, and Genia read it through. "There's nothing written here that could cause offence. Aha! So you're the Pacifist Society of Brutalia! We heard about you when we stopped for a fresh pawpaw juice on Dead Man's Island."

Mort felt his heart pitter-pat. They'd been to Dead Man's Island? That wonderful sloping rock with its terraces of flowers and its bars of cheery sailors?

"Did you meet my friend Ono Assunder?" Mort's face was ripe with hope.

Vita laughed. "Yes! Who do you think gave me this haircut? Not too short, I said, but then we got chatting, and the next thing I know – I look like Ono!"

Mort smiled and nodded, although Vita could never look like Ono. Ono was one of a kind.

"In fact, Ono gave me a note to deliver. It's addressed to *Mort Canal*."

"That's me!"

Mort took the note. Last time he'd seen Ono was in Book One, but if you haven't read it then a) make your own note that says *go and read Book One*, and b) let's cut to the chase: Ono was interesting and wise and had taught Mort that not everything is black and white (apart from most species of penguin). What wisdom could she possibly be imparting now?

**Hi, Mort. Hope there's a plot to this story. Love Ono**

Mort wiped away a tear. "Something needs to happen now," he said. "Perhaps it's to do with you two."

"I doubt it. I sent my toucan back with a message to bring a vessel. It'll be here at dawn to collect us," Genia said.

"So you're not really part of this story?"

"Afraid not."

There was a shuffling outside the window. They all froze.

"Probably just a pigeon," Weed said.

Probably wasn't just a pigeon, though... It was a good job the girls were leaving the story.

44

That night, under the cloak of darkness, Genia and Vita crept back to the coast to meet their boat and return to Bonrock. No one saw them apart from an old man, wrinkly as a paper bag and as forgetful as a thingummy, who was taking his pet rat for a late-night wee.

*Who's that under the cloak of darkness?* he wondered, before wondering why he was outside in his pyjamas, holding a rat on a string.

So the girls got away, and that's the last we'll see of them.

# CHAPTER FIVE
# SHUCKS!

*"Have you ever thought about
joining the forces, Ratto?"*

*"I already have, Ratty.
The forces of evil."*

The room was full of guards carrying pointy sticks, and in the middle of them the Queen sat on a sofa made of spider velvet. She was reclining as one might on a Sunday afternoon with a box of chocolates. Only she was slurping from a bowl of oysters. She sucked up the poor little creatures and threw their shells over her shoulder, where they clattered on the stone floor behind.

This went on for some time. *Shuck, pluck, slurp, clatter.* (To create an air of tension.) She was also looking for pearls (but having no luck as Salty Sea oysters could rarely be bothered to make them). The Queen was obsessed with gemstones, of which there were none in Brutalia. Drill a mine and the best you'd find were lumps of brown. Which is also the worst you'd find.

Kneeling before the royal slurper were Mort and Weed. And they knew exactly why they were there, thanks to the presence of Snit Parlot. He greased around in the background with his arms folded behind his back, his smug eyes orbiting the room and watering with joy. Oh yes, he was very pleased with himself.

The Queen popped an oyster on her tongue and looked accusingly at Mort. "It's you again. Why is it **ALWAYS** you?"

Mort raised an eyebrow that said, *Do we really need to explain why a book called* Mort the Meek *always involves a boy called Mort the Meek?*

The Queen rolled her eyes. "Whatever. It has come to my attention that there have been strangers on the shore. Strangers are not welcome. They have **NEVER** been welcome. But why are they **VERY NOT WELCOME** at this moment?"

"Because of the Soup Prophecy," Mort answered, wondering where this was going and not liking the direction.

"Correct. **Drats 'n' rats!**"

You thought she'd have been happy with a correct answer, but there's no pleasing some people.

"So you *were* there at the square. Can't punish you for non-attendance, then. YES, the **PROPHECY** from the Royal Soup Sayer. And yet you did what?"

Mort and Weed were in a tight spot. If they admitted meeting strangers, then they'd be thrown in a hot bog. If they didn't admit it, they might still be thrown in a hot bog. They were in a whole swamp of trouble either way, but the Queen was enjoying the sound of her own voice and thundered on.

"Oh, I know all about you boys!" she cried. "I've had to beef up my security because of you!"

"I don't think you need to worry about these stra—" Mort began.

"Oh REALLY!" the Queen squealed, eyes a-goggling. "He says I don't have to worry! Never mind the soup – Mort the Meek says it's all OK. But it's **NOT OK!**" she yelled. "Tell us what you overheard, Parlot."

"*Misheard, more like,*" Weed whispered under his breath.

Snit Parlot sped to her side. "Your Majesty, I heard one of the strange girls say, '*We sent a tin can home with a message to bring a wrestle.*'"

"A *wrestle!*" the Queen shouted. "A **wrestle**, if I'm not mistaken, is another word for tussle, which is another word for **struggle**, which is another word for fight, which is another word for WAR!"

Weed looked at Mort with a look that said, *Blimey, she sure knows her synonyms!*\*

"Your Majesty, they sent a **toucan** with a message for a **vessel**," Mort explained. "The boat they came in got smashed on the rocks."

"And rightly so!" the Queen shrieked. "Even our rocks know not to let in strangers, which is more than I can say for you! And we know all about their boat... Marcus Sucram!"

Marcus heaved one of the boat's wooden planks into the centre of the room. The one that had writing in fancy lettering, but not too fancy.

"*Packs Navy*," she hissed. "What sort of packs? Weapon packs? Poison packs? Packs of evil rats? It couldn't sound more fiendish if it tried."

Mort coughed. "You don't know that. It might be

another language. It could be pronounced differently...
Or it could mean *Peace Boat* in Latin."

"Don't tell me what I don't know," she spat.
"What I do know is that you boys made them feel
**WELCOME**. They'll tell all their friends that
Brutalians are as soft as porridge, and strangers will be
swarming in with plans to steal our food and eat our
children and rob us of our ancient customs."

"They might be happy with their own customs—"
Mort began.

"You boys are in **BIG** trouble. And that calls for a
punishment!"

Weed looked at Mort with a look that said, *Oops.*

Mort returned the look, with an extra letter. *Woops.*

Snit tittered until the Queen shoved him. Then he
teetered.

"Shut up. I haven't finished. As I was saying,
this calls for punishment... HOWEVER, we have
something else in mind. Bring Throt Gutsem!"

Marcus Sucram hollered like a mountain's echo.

# "THROT GUTSEM!"

The doors were flung open, and the Battle-Chief entered. He'd oiled his muscles so they shone like newborn baby cows. He snapped open a piece of paper and began to read.

"Mort Canal and Weed Millet, we are relieving you of all punishment."

"That's a relief," Weed said, puffing out his cheeks.

"Instead, you are immediately enrolled in the Brutalian Army. Due to the urgency of the operation of which I am about to inform you, there will be no formal training. You are, effective as of now, on duty. *Atteeeeeention!*"

"I think you've already got our attention," Mort said, staring glumly at the man's breastplate which was carved with the words **War is Great**.

Throt's chin shook. "When I say,

*Atteeeeeention!*, it means

stand tall. Let's try it again, shall we? *Atteeeeeention!*"

Mort and Weed stood tall, Mort a bit taller as he had his hand in the air.

"What is it, boy?"

"I'm afraid we'll have to take the punishment instead. We can't join the army. We are pacifists who don't believe in violence."

"What do you mean you don't believe in violence?" Throt couldn't swallow his disbelief, so he spat it out on to Mort and Weed. "You can't not believe in something that exists. I'd like not to believe in pimples, but it doesn't stop me having a rather painful one on my backside right now."

"I understand," Mort said carefully. "And I'm sorry to hear about your spotty bum, but when I say I don't believe in it I mean I don't believe in doing it, and I don't believe there's an excuse for it. Violence is not fun."

Throt put his hands on his hips. Then he laughed a rich, gutsy laugh that made their eyes ache and their bones vibrate.

"Ah, my boy, you've never experienced the thrill of the chase, the excitement of closing in on your enemy.

Then there are the stages – the strategy stage, the stealth stage, the stage where you smell victory."

"I can live without it," Mort said defiantly.

Throt gave his big laugh again, and the boys felt that this might, in fact, be a worse punishment than a hot bog with added ingredients.

## *"Atteeeeeention!"*

The boys snapped themselves upright and lifted their chins. Throt Gutsem slowly circled them.

"Since I was a little boy, I dreamed of doing something honourable with my life, and nothing is more honourable than protecting your homeland. So I trained hard, prepared myself mentally and physically for the time when my loyalty would be put to the test. I lifted rocks to make my muscles as big as baby cows, and I played out battles in my sleep. And finally, FINALLY, the day has come. Strangers are invading, and I'm ready for 'em. I've been ready my whole life." Throt held his head high.

"That's a really nice story," Mort said, "but we cannot be a part of it."

"And you don't have to be." The Battle-Chief's

steely eyes shone. "You see, I have a plan. A plan that has two halves. And the first half involves no violence whatsoever."

"That sounds all right, doesn't it, Mort?" Weed said hopefully.

"What about the second half?" Mort asked.

"We'll cross that bridge if you're still alive to cross it."

# CHAPTER SIX
# THE SNORTY NANCY

*"There's something suspicious
going on here. I smell a rat."*

*"Me too, Ratto, me too…"*

In the middle of the Salty Sea, a creaky ship called the *Snorty Nancy* was navigating the dangers and deadly currents on its way to Bonrock Island. On board were the Brutalian Army's newest recruits and a raven called Roger. It's not clear if Roger was queasy, but Mort and Weed definitely were. And they weren't sure if it was because of the violent grey seas or the briefing they'd just been given by Throt Gutsem.

Vita and Genia were nice – perhaps a bit too clever – but they were also friendly and interesting and definitely not the sort to scheme. At least **that's what Mort and Weed had thought**... But then, during their briefing, Throt said things that crawled into their brains like maggots of mistrust, making them

wonder if they actually knew anything about the few things they thought they did know, which is awfully confusing.

"I don't know what to think any more!" Mort wailed as he paced the deck of the *Snorty Nancy*.

He'd wailed it so many times that Roger had picked up a few words and shouted them repeatedly, like an overcaffeinated parrot. "*Know more! Know more!*"

"And, if Throt's right about Bonrock, we could be saving lives, and that's good, isn't it?" Weed said, hoping to be helpful.

"I don't know," Mort sobbed.

Right now, you're probably as confused as a cockle in a cocktail. So here is Throt Gutsem's briefing scene written down as a play for dramatic effect (because Throt just loves a bit of drama):

Location: a room somewhere in the Royal Palace, a few hours earlier.

MORT and WEED are standing to attention. THROT GUTSEM is pointing to two large drawings on the wall. In the first picture, boats are pulling into the docks. In the second picture, there are people on the ground with their mouths open, being trodden on, and there are guts everywhere. THROT is a terrible artist and the guts look like small garden worms. THROT turns to the boys.

THROT GUTSEM:
You see strangers arriving in the first picture. We think they just want to borrow a cup of instant coffee or some sugar. But wait! What is happening in the second picture?

WEED MILLET:
Are we stamping on the strangers and making them sing songs to our worms?

THROT GUTSEM:
No, you fool. The strangers are stamping on US, making us SCREAM — that's screaming, not singing — and they're not worms, they're GUTS. They are OUR guts, spilled on the ground of our OWN country by strangers who do not want to borrow anything at all. They want to TAKE IT. Mort, I think you'd better be team leader.

MORT CANAL:
So long as I don't have to do any
violence.

THROT GUTSEM:
Let's look at the pictures again.
Strangers arrive then stamp our guts
out. Strangers are bad.

MORT CANAL:
But we can't be sure. The two girls we
met seemed nice.

THROT GUTSEM:
They SEEMED nice? You cannot trust
anyone. What were they doing here in
the first place? Did you even ask?

WEED MILLET:
Of course we did! They were collecting
information on Brutalia for a project.

THROT GUTSEM:
A project! And how do you know this
project wasn't to gather vital
information about Brutalia so they can
attack it? They now know the layout of
our island, how it works, what we do.
Don't you know? Knowledge is power...

THE END

Let's get back to our story.

### "KNOW MORE!
### KNOW MORE!
### KNOW MORE!"

"You're not helping, Roger," Mort sighed.

"There it is." Weed's eyes turned to the horizon where the shape of a large island was forming in the mist. "Bonrock. Who knows what's waiting for us?"

"With any luck, it's a lovely place, and Throt's got it all wrong."

"But, if he's right, then we do as he said – we wait until the Bonrockians are off guard and send Roger as a signal to attack... Can we do that and still be pacifists, Mort?"

Mort gulped. "We'll peel that potato when we come to it. The first thing to worry about is whether Bonrockians will welcome us in peace. We don't know what Vita and Genia told them after their experience on Brutalia. They might not be pleased to see us."

They sailed on, unsure of what was going to happen next. Roger the Raven occasionally yelled out caws of confusion, and a toucan yelled out croaks of—

*HOLD ON. A TOUCAN?*

Mort gasped. "It must be the one Vita lost!"

"Let's have a look," Weed said.

He crawled inside the cabin where a toucan
was cowering, soggy and salty from its dunking at
Crashbang Cove.

"Come here, little fella," Weed said, extending the
hand of kindness.

The toucan extended its alarmingly colourful beak
and snapped at his finger.

"OW, Mort!" Weed said, shooting back on to the
deck. "That toucan is terrible. Nasty. If that's how
Bonrock trains its pets, then this is not a good sign."

They looked up to see if there were any more bad
signs, but ahead was a calm turquoise sea. They were
entering tropical waters, and Bonrock was getting
larger and larger.

A harbour emerged – a bite-shaped bight that
housed gangways and moorings and ships that looked
sturdy and unsinkable. Mort thought of Brutalia's
docks with its rickety boats made from cabbage crates
and its high death toll due to people slipping straight

into the open mouths of salty sharks. They certainly did things differently here.

"What if they see the *Snorty Nancy* and think we're attacking?" Weed asked worriedly.

"Yes. If only there was a way to let them know we come in peace..."

**"Ahoy there!"**

They looked over the side of the boat to see a small girl in a canoe bobbing alongside. She had dark brown skin and long straight hair down to her knees, and she was holding a sandwich.

"Er, hi there!" Mort said. "Do you live on Bonrock?"

"No, I'm a floating trader."

"You trade sandwiches?" Weed licked his lips.

The girl giggled. "This is my lunch, silly! I don't trade anything of my own – I get islands to talk and trade with each other, and they give me little things in return. I'm Ngoshi."

"Pleased to meet you, Ngoshi. Can you tell us – is Bonrock a good place?"

"Oh yes, full of opals, pearls and rubies. Very good for me." She pulled back her curtain of hair and flashed shiny pearl earrings. "I'm on my way to broker a deal for Jaundice Island. They want to sell their bananas to Bonrock in return for opals. What are you bringing to trade?"

"We're bringing a war—"

"Warm greeting," Mort interrupted quickly. "For now," he added for honesty's sake. "Ngoshi, could you possibly go on ahead and tell them that we come in peace?"

Ngoshi held out her hand and wriggled her fingers. "What can you give me?"

Weed checked his pockets. "Two clams and a lump of brown stuff."

"Better than *one* clam and a lump of brown stuff, I guess. Sure, OK. I'll head off after my lunch."

Mort and Weed dropped anchor, and Ngoshi ate her sandwich.

# CHAPTER SEVEN
# LAND OF CONFUSION

*"What are we even doing
in this story, Ratto?"*

*"We're embodying the spirit
of the two nations –*

*I'm Bonrock because I'm clever, and
you're Brutalia because you stink."*

Ngoshi sailed off to Bonrock and returned not long after with a big thumbs up.

"Are they happy for us to visit?" Mort asked.

"Oh yes. Everything's OK!" she called. "And I love my new clip-on earrings!" She pulled back her curtain of hair to reveal Weed's two clams, now clamped to her pretty earlobes. "Cool, huh? Now follow me!"

She guided the *Snorty Nancy* into the harbour (where she disappeared to make her trades), and people with twinkly eyes and clean skin and smiles that revealed full sets of teeth lined the boardwalks to greet the boys of Brutalia.

"It's Mort and Weed! Make them welcome!"

The strong voices of Vita and Genia soared over the crowd, and Mort spotted them pushing through to the front of the quayside.

Weed shot Mort a petrified look. "I don't like this one bit." He sniffed the air. "It smells off."

"It smells fine, Weed. You've probably just got a hermit crab up your nose." Mort picked a small sea slug from his leg and popped it back into the water.

"No, it doesn't smell of anything. That's the

problem. It's just weird."

Weed plucked a bottle of **Eau de Errr** (Brutalia's only perfume) from his tunic and gave his surroundings a good spritz. "That's better."

They threw the mooring ropes on to the quayside, where lithe Bonrockians leaped over each other like frogs to pull the ropes tight and tether the *Snorty Nancy* securely.

"It's OK, Weed. It's going to be OK."

"I-I-I don't know, Mort," Weed stuttered, looking at the toucan bite on his finger. "I'm so confused."

"Greetings!" In one graceful bound, Vita sprang on to the deck. "Welcome to Bonrock! We're so pleased to see you!"

"Why are you glad we came?" Weed asked suspiciously.

"Because we like you," Vita laughed. "Are you doing a project too?"

"Um, sort of," Mort said, which wasn't a lie.

Vita helped them off the boat and on to dry land, where Genia was talking to some grown-ups, who nodded and stroked their chins, like wise people do.

"It's decided," Genia called. "Vita and I will be your guides. First, let's— What's that dreadful smell? It reminds me of the Mists of Despair we encountered around Brutalia. They must have been very thick today. You poor boys, having to sail through that!"

Mort motioned for Weed to put the bottle of **Eau de Errr** away. "It must have clung to the boat," he said.

"Not to worry. We'll get your boat cleaned, and we'll have a bubble bath drawn for our weary travellers."

Mort and Weed looked at each other in alarm. If Bonrockians could draw things into existence, then they hoped Vita was a better artist than Throt Gutsem.

Genia saw their confusion. "To draw a bath means to run one. Do you have baths on Brutalia? Come to think of it – and I really do think a lot – we didn't see any, did we, Vita?"

"We do have a bath," Mort said.

It wasn't a lie – he had once seen one in the square filled with cabbages and a sign saying LUCKY DIP (it turned out there were scorpions in the bottom).

"Come on! We've so much to show you!" Vita squealed.

She and Genia skipped away, and Mort and Weed tried to follow, but, compared to the gazelle-like girls, they were as slow as well-fed slugs.

"I think they've drugged us," Weed said, panting. "We've been poisoned!"

Mort whispered, *"I think they're just ... healthy."*

Suddenly two hands slipped into theirs. The girls were back, laughing and pulling them so they bounced along behind like prize cabbages at the Annual Cabbage

Drag. They eventually arrived at a large stone house, and Weed stopped abruptly, hand pointing shakily to a sign nailed to the wall.

"What's the matter?" Mort said.

"Hostile," Weed mumbled. "They're going to murder us – or worse!"

Mort sighed and wished that Leggo Mentis had managed to teach literacy to a few more people before he'd agreed to play Do-or-die Tiddlywinks.

"It says *hostel*, Weed. A place to stay."

"Oh right." He cheered up a bit after that.

The boys were given a room with two large beds and a separate bathroom, where Genia was already drawing them a bath without using a single pencil. The smell of soapy steam tickled their nostrils with its unfamiliar suggestion of hygiene.

The girls left them alone to get refreshed, and Mort and Weed found themselves laughing stupidly.

"Why am I giggling?" Weed said, going pale. "Do you think they've put a spell on me?"

"Perhaps it's because, for the first time in your life, you're COMFORTABLE."

Mort had experienced a brief period of comfort when he stayed with Ono Assunder on Dead Man's Island. He'd never forgotten the soft bed and the clean, bugless sheets – not to mention the cuddly chinchilla. He was disappointed not to see one here, but the chocolate on a rolled-up towel was a nice touch.

When they were as clean as absolutely nothing on Brutalia was, they ventured out of the Bonrock Hostel to discover Vita and Genia waiting for them astride two magnificent stallions.

"Ready for a tour?" Vita reached down for Mort's hand and pulled him up.

Genia did the same with Weed and, with a click of the girls' tongues, the steeds began to trot and then gallop, and Weed started to wail.

"This is torture!" he cried. "Just kill me now!"

"Try moving to the rhythm of the horse," Vita shouted. "*Up-up-down. Up-up-down.*"

Weed looked over at Mort and grinned. "I'm alive!" he said, getting a hang of the *up-up-downing*.

"It does make you feel alive, doesn't it!" said Genia, who as well as having a cute face also had acute* hearing. "Let's go faster!"

They flew (not literally – they weren't unicorns) over the green countryside, stopping at viewpoints to look down at beautiful beaches. The water didn't seem to have the same grey fury as the Salty Sea, with its angry spits and choppy top. It was aquamarine with a surface as flat as a crab's back. But it wasn't crabby at all. On it bobbed little pleasure boats – boats that took to the water just for fun – and Weed and Mort couldn't believe their eyes. The boats in Brutalia were *displeasure* boats – they were covered in slime and held together with grime and tossed like boat-shaped pancakes on the choppy waves.

As they trotted along the coastal path, their hair was flicked tenderly by a soft, happy breeze. The absence of horribleness was intoxicating, and the boys' worries vanished like puppies* in a Grot Bear's cage.

---

*Homophone bingo! A homophone is a word that sounds like another word, which can get you into trouble as you'll know if you've ever made faces at a guerrilla. (A GORILLA is an ape. A GUERRILLA is a soldier.)

---

**No puppies were harmed in the making of this simile.

"Where are all the other children?" Mort said.

Apart from the two clever girls, there was no one else their age around.

"They're doing what all of us should be doing – learning," said Genia. "Come on, we'll show you."

They turned the horses to face inland and followed a path to a place where there were plenty of Bonrockian children. A whole field of them in fact.

The sight thwacked Mort and Weed in the face like a surprise wet rat. They had been lulled into a sense of security by Scenic Tours on Horseback, but at the sight of this dreadful spectacle the ugly undercurrent of Throt's briefing returned, and pictures of people with wormy guts flashed before their eyes. For this was a place of utter horror.

There were fences round the perimeter of the field to stop the children from running away, and inside guards were **TORTURING** them.

Tongues frozen and eyes prickling, Mort and Weed watched aghast as the children were forced to run and jump and then lie down and get up again. Some grunted and some even asked to stop. But they weren't

allowed to – they had to keep going. Grown-ups
with armless shirts and legless trousers stood like
mini battle-chiefs, their sinewy muscles as tight as
strings. Mort and Weed had seen biceps before on
the likes of Lance Pollip, Marcus Sucram and Throt
Gutsem, but these ones weren't bulgy like baby cows.
They were small and quick, wriggling beneath the skin
like eels. They were like a totally different species of
muscle.

"Are you enjoying the show?" Vita asked. "Watch
this – it'll be good."

Mort and Weed did watch, with horror, as a grown-
up shouted, and a row of small children lined up. They
looked tense and on edge.

Then the grown-up held something in the air that
went...

# BANG!

Scared out of their wits, the children ran a perfect
hundred-metre sprint. One sped far ahead of the
others, and he would certainly have won a cabbage
drag race if only he'd been pulling a cabbage on a string.
As he wasn't, it was clearly **TORTURE**.

Weed edged closer to Mort. "Are you thinking what I'm thinking?"

Mort's heart was racing. "What are you thinking?"

"While they're busy torturing children, they won't be prepared for battle. It could be now or never. Shall we go back to the *Snorty Nancy* and let Roger loose?"

Mort bit his lip. If they set Roger free, it would give the signal for Throt to attack. And that would mean violence.

"We *can't*," he whispered. "*The Pacifist Promise, Weed. Oh, what shall we do?*"

"Why don't we just go?" Weed said. "Set sail and think up an excuse to never come back."

He widened his large chocolatey eyes, and Mort regarded them a while with his average-sized green ones.

"That's a really good idea. Leave the talking to me."

Vita and Genia were now cheering as the last child in the scaredy-sprint got to the other end of the field, where she collapsed and rolled on the ground dramatically.

Vita turned to Mort. "Such a good sport!" she

declared. "A fine example of what a human can do."

Oh, humans could torture all right. Mort didn't need to be convinced of that. He'd seen plenty of Brutalians forced to do terrifying acts in the name of the Queen – like leaping into pits of dung or eating urchins with the spikes still on. Sometimes at the same time.

Mort momentarily considered pretending that he had to nip back to the ship to get something, but honesty was always the best policy. "Vita, we want to go home now."

"Really?" she said disappointedly. "But there's so much more to show you! The classrooms and the kitchens... Your project won't be complete without seeing those. And there's nothing worse than a half-baked project."

"I have an idea," said Genia. "Why don't I take Weed to the classrooms, and you can take Mort to the kitchens? That way, we'll kill two birds with one stone. Then you can leave, knowing everything."

*Are we the birds?* Weed mouthed.

*Do we want to know everything?* Mort wondered.

# CHAPTER EIGHT
# THE DIN-DIN OF DOOM

"What are we doing in this story, Bruce?"

"I don't know. But I wish we
weren't in a kitchen, Larry."

"Yeah, for starters, being a
chef is hard work."

"When it comes to starters, being
a lobster is worse."

As Vita pulled Mort towards the kitchens, he was on high alert. And he quickly became alerter (which is not a real word as Genia will tell you) – MORE ALERT (that's better) – when he heard the sound of blades being sharpened, along with metallic crashes.

"That's why we call it din-dins," Vita laughed. She waited. "Get it? Din. Din?" She regarded Mort pityingly. "Don't you have jokes on Brutalia? Oh, you poor things. Let's see if we can get some good Bonrockian humour into you before you go. *If you go!*" She grinned and Mort's heart began to canter.

**IF YOU GO...**

**If you go** had all sorts of bad intentions:

**IF YOU GO** DOWN TO THE WOODS TODAY, YOU'RE SURE TO BE AMBUSHED.

(*traditional nursery rhyme*)

**IF YOU GO** BEFORE I'VE FINISHED TALKING, I'LL PICKLE YOUR TONGUE.

(*the Queen*)

**IF YOU GO,** YOUR BACK WILL BE TURNED AND WE'LL ATTACK!

(*Mort's vivid imagination*)

But the most likely meaning of this one was:

**IF YOU GO** – with the emphasis on the **IF** – meaning there's a probability you'll never get out of here alive because...

**"THE CHEESE SAUCE IS TOO RUNNY!"**

Life and death didn't depend on the consistency of cheese sauce. It's just what the Bonrockian chef happened to be shouting at that very moment.

Mort looked at the faces of the cooks who'd been yelled at. They didn't seem confused or scared. Instead, they nodded like brainwashed parrots.

**"Chef, yes, chef!"**

**"SOMEONE CHECK THE SOUFFLÉS!"**

**"Chef, yes, chef!"**

"Why do the soufflés need checking?" Mort feared some kind of torture instrument, like a whistling blade or bellows that pumped you full of air until you popped.

"If the cooks don't follow the chef's instructions, it'll be a disaster," Vita explained.

This did not put Mort's mind at rest – probably because Vita did not point out that:

• soufflés were puffy little puddings and NOT some

kind of whipping device, and

• they were very tricky to make, and

• the disaster would not befall the chefs but the
puffy little puddings, which would deflate like a
porcupine's armbands.

"Come and meet our head chef," Vita said excitedly.
"Mort, this is Coochina Sapori."

When Coochina emerged from the steam of a large
tureen, Mort saw a woman who was taller than a small
horse with a large face. (If you think that sentence
needs a comma, then go ahead and put one in.)
Her long grey hair was tied in a neat bun at the
nape of her neck. Her
blue eyes twinkled like
wet cockles. But although
her presence was
overwhelming, and the
kitchen smells were
lip-smackingly delicious,
it's what was inside
her pot that caught
Mort's eye.

A blood-red soup. And in Coochina's huge hands, about to be tossed into the bubbling turmoil, were three large, squidgy, crimson hearts. At the sight of such horror, his insides twisted.

"I d-don't feel well," Mort said, trying not to throw up in the nearest pan.

"Get him out of the kitchens, quickly!" Coochina Sapori boomed. "Health and safety!"

"Don't worry about Coochina," Vita said kindly, leading Mort away. "Chefs are always a little bit snappy. They have so much to do that their conversation is short. They don't really have time to stir in pleasantries."

"You eat peasants?" Mort gasped, boggle-eyed, and clutched his stomach.

"No, I said PLEASANTRIES – it means friendly conversation. But I assure you the chef is very nice. Heartily so."

*Heartily.* GULP!

"Oh dear, Mort, you do look pale. I'll take you back to the hostel for a rest and see if I can find Genia and Weed."

Back at the hostel, Mort sat on his bed and waited for Weed to arrive. He nibbled the nails on every finger and toe, wondering if he would ever scrub the image of heart soup from his eyes. This island was a revolting concoction of all that Mort despised – violence, torture and wickedness hiding behind a friendly face. Oh, cruel deception!

A few minutes later, the door was flung open, and Weed rushed in. He wrapped his arms round Mort like an amorous octopus.

"Mort! Mort! Thank goodness you're alive!" he panted. "When Genia said that you were probably stuffing yourself in the kitchen, I imagined the worst. I thought they were going to cook you, Mort!"

Mort pulled his friend to the corner of the room and put his fingers against his lips. "Shh. Be calm."

"They didn't cook you, did they?" Weed checked Mort for signs of singeing or cleaving.

"Weed, tell me what you saw when you went off with Genia."

"Well, first of all, I saw her lovely hair and how it blew in the wind like a horse's mane..."

Weed's dreamy expression suddenly vanished, and his chin wobbled as he explained what came next – the tour of the places they called 'classrooms', where children sat in rows like little armies, looking straight ahead as so-called 'teachers' pointed at words and pictures on a board.

"I don't think they're teachers. I think they're army generals. One of them was pointing to a map of Brutalia. I think ... they're going to *attack* us, Mort!"

Mort opened his mouth to speak, but, while the maggots of mistrust wriggled furiously, no words crawled out.

"But why would they attack us?" Weed pondered. "We don't have anything worth taking. Our island is ugly. They hate the smell. Unless they really like lumps of brown, it doesn't make any sense."

"Weed, when I tell you what I'm about to tell you, you have to promise not to scream."

"I promise."

"Promise there'll be no screaming?"

"No screaming. I promise."

Mort leaned into his friend's ear and whispered,

*"I think they eat hearts."*

# "ARRRRRGHGHGHGHGHHHGHGH!"

Vita and Genia rushed in.

"What's the matter?" Vita was flustered.

"Weed stubbed his toe, that's all," Mort said hurriedly. "But it's OK now."

# "ARRRGHGHGHGHGHGHGHGHHG!"

"Then why is he still screaming?" Genia said, putting her hands over her ears.

"Should I call the doctor?" Vita shouted over the noise.

Weed's eyes were wild with panic, and he was staring at the girls as if they might morph into demons at any moment. The two boys hadn't had enough time to think up a plan, and Mort hoped with all his might that Weed wouldn't go and say something that got them into trouble.

# "ARRRGHGHGHGHGHGHGHGHHG!"

"Calm down, calm down," said Genia soothingly. She approached Weed with her hands up, palms outwards, and placed them on his chest. "It's going to be OK."

Weed pushed her away, eyes bulging. "DON'T EAT MY HEART!"

There was a silence that, if it had had lips, would have sucked up everything in the room.

The girls stood like confused statues, and the boys cowered like frightened sea cucumbers.

Genia put her hands on her hips. "Why did he say that? Why did he think I was going to *eat his heart*?"

Mort, sticking with honesty being the best policy, un-cowered himself and stood tall. "I saw them in your kitchens. Hearts. Blood-red hearts. And we don't approve. Because we're pacifists. And also because we don't want to be eaten."

Vita and Genia looked at each other. Then they tipped their heads back and laughed. And never had such a pretty sound sounded so cruel and ugly.

# CHAPTER NINE
# THE WRONG END OF THE STICK

*"I'd eat anything, me. Anything at all."*

*"Even hearts?"*

*"Nah, they taste offal."*

**"TOR-MAY-DOH!"**

**"TOH-MAR-TOE!"**

**"TOE-MAH-DOH!"**

"There are lots of ways of saying it," Vita said, "but we tend to pronounce it **t'marto**."

"You just made that up!" Weed protested.

Mort thought it sounded made up too. But Vita and Genia had befuddled them with so many new words, how were they to know what was a real word and what was just a cacophony?*

"I didn't make it up. A tomato is a vegetable—"

"A fruit," Genia corrected. "It has seeds inside, so technically it's a fruit."

"Do you put tomato in a fruit salad? No, you don't. It's used like a vegetable," Vita insisted. "So if we're going to define it by its purpose, which, for the sake of helping the boys understand, we should, then I suggest we call it a vegetable."

Weed and Mort listened to the conversation going back and forth in awe and fear, as if they were watching unicorns playing tennis with a bomb.

---

*Pronounced 'cack-off-oh-knee', it's a real word meaning lots of noise.

"What do you think, Mort?"

Mort blinked as if he had millipedes on his eyelids. "Vita, I don't care if it's a fruit or a vegetable. What I care about is whether you're telling the truth or not. Because to me they look very much like human hearts."

"Is that a Brutalian joke? You are funny! Funny as in peculiar, that is. Come on. Let's introduce you to the finest veget—"

"Fruit," Genia corrected.

"How about we call it a fruitable?" Weed suggested helpfully.

Vita beamed. "Language is always evolving, and you, my dear Weed, are a genius. From now on, the tomato will be a **fruitable**."

"You can call it what you want, but it'll still be a fruit," Genia said, with a shrug. "Can't ignore the science."

Vita laughed gaily. "Don't mind her – she's such a stickler for facts. Let's go to the kitchens, and we'll show you a tomato close up."

They were going to take them to the place of din and sharp dissecting knives? That sounded like a trap.

Mort shook his head.

"All right, then, if you won't come to the tomatoes, then we'll bring the tomatoes to you," Genia said. "Sit outside in the sunshine, and we'll be back shortly."

The girls rode off on their stallions, with laughter billowing behind them.

"They're making fun of us," Weed tutted.

"Let's just hope that's all they make of us," Mort said.

The girls returned minutes later with a large basket. Inside was something called a **PICNIC**, which sounded even more like a torture instrument than all the other things that sounded like torture instruments.

But a **PICNIC** turned out to be little bits of food.

*"Shouldn't it be a* **BIT-PICK***?"* Weed whispered. *"If they're going to invent words, they should at least make sense."*

The picnic/bit-pick was bread, olive oil, salt and the curious, dubious fruitables called **TUR-MAR-TERS** (that's another way of saying it).

"Go on, touch one," Vita said, with a slightly wicked grin, which didn't go unnoticed.

"Did you see her wicked grin?" Weed whispered, nudging Mort. "Don't touch it. Don't!"

Mort sat on his hands and stared at the fruitable.

"That one looks like a bit like a derrière, a behind, a posterior, don't you think, boys?" Genia giggled.

"A BUM," Vita added, her twinkly eyes teasing them.

"Oooh, Sally McRoot would LOVE that, wouldn't she? Wouldn't she, Mort? A vegetable shaped like a bum?" Weed said, excited by the discovery and awed by Genia's mastery of synonyms.

But, while Mort could certainly see the object's bottomy characteristics, he also saw its vital-organy ones.

"Touch it," Genia said. "It won't bite."

Mort carefully extended his finger and, with a push of determination, jabbed the tomato. It didn't squish. In fact, the exterior was surprisingly firm.

"See?" Vita produced a sharp knife and began slicing it into fine translucent discs that spread like rose petals over the plate. And inside was a clear liquid. And seeds.

Mort gasped. "So this means..."

"IT'S A FRUIT!" Weed yelled, high-fiving Genia.

"...that it's not a heart," Mort finished. **"It's not a heart!"**

The relief that swept through him made him want to dance and sing, but there were still questions to be asked. (And answered, obviously.)

"So perhaps you don't want to eat our hearts," he said, "but there's plenty more things that need explaining."

"Like what?" asked Vita.

She placed a sliver of tomato on to a piece of bread, drizzled oil and a sprinkle of salt on top and pushed it against Mort's mouth.

"Like ... **FRUMPDDCRUMPH**... Oh my goodness, that flavour!"

"And here's the tomato in soup form," Genia said, lifting a spoon to his lips. In it was a dollop of the red squish he'd mistaken for blood.

Flavours shot through his tongue like an arrow through a rotten cabbage, only faster and tastier.

"This is SO good!" he said to Weed, who was busy scoffing oily bread and hearty tomatoes and was totally lost in the deliciousness.

The girls were looking at each other funny. Funny ha-ha or funny peculiar?

"Stop distracting us," Mort said. "Tell us why you are torturing children and planning to attack Brutalia."

"Torturing children?" Vita questioned.

"Planning to attack Brutalia?" Genia quizzed.

"We saw children forced to bend their bodies into painful shapes," Weed said. "And you stood there, like it was a sport."

"It WAS a sport," Vita said. "And the kids that were being tortured... Is that them over there?"

The children, still in their ~~torture~~ sport clothes, came laughing and dancing over the hill, eating strawberries and singing traditional Bonrockian songs like:

'If You're Happy and You Know It, Then You Must Be on Bonrock'

'It's Only Bonrock 'n' Roll But I Like It'

'Heads, Shoulders, Knees and Toes (all mechanically sound and in peak condition)'

"I love the hundred-metres sprint race!" shouted one, just to rub it in.

"My strength is maths," said another. "But I still love to keep fit."

"What you saw was an athletics lesson. It's to improve fitness," Genia explained. "We believe in healthy bodies and healthy minds. We noticed on Brutalia that you were all weak and spindly – so I'm guessing you don't do any physical training?"

Weed leaped to his feet. "All right, so forget about the tomatoes that weren't hearts and the athletics lessons that weren't tortures. Why were those troops of children looking at a map of Brutalia if you're not planning an attack?"

Genia shook her head, and her long waves of hair shimmered round her face like a chestnut mirage. "Those schoolchildren were learning about the geography of the Salty Sea, and they were discussing how clever Brutalia is to survive in such a place. Your ability to stay alive – it's a brilliant example of how humans find a way to survive. You're very tenacious – *TEN-AY-SHUS*. It means good at not giving up. Brutalia is part of the curriculum now, thanks to our project. We got top marks, by the way."

"Oh, well done," Weed said, his eyes now a bit starry.

"So you weren't gathering information for an attack?" Mort wanted absolute confirmation of that.

"No, no, no," Vita chuckled. "It really was just a geography project and, although we think you live like cockroaches and smell like a thousand demon farts, we are in awe of you. Bonrockians might be beautiful, strong and intelligent, but we wouldn't survive a day on that strange island of yours."

"Thank you," Weed said, still gazing adoringly.

"What would we want to attack you for anyway?" Genia added, fluttering her eyelids sweetly. "We're pacifists! Didn't we tell you? Oh, Vita – we forgot to tell them!"

"You're pacifists?" Weed and Mort gasped.

"Then what are we waiting for? Let's relax and enjoy Bonrock!" Weed tugged at the girls' sleeves.

"Time for a Bonrock montage," Mort agreed.

# DREAMY

**Mort spots a new
variety of marigold...**
"What a wonderful place this is!"
Mort cried, leaping into a patch
of blooms with petals so
bright they shone like
little orange suns.

**Weed plays with a friendly creature...**
"Hey there, little fellow. What is this
creature that looks so sweet?"
"It's a vampire rat," said Genia.
"Don't scare him, Genia!" Vita laughed.
The chipmunk laughed too, and
soon they were all rolling around,
clutching their tummies.

# MONTAGE

**They frolic in the crystal streams of Bonrock...**

"I'm skimming stones, Weed. Come
and see!" Mort shouted with delight
as he flicked his pebble across the little
river, making it hop like a stony frog.
"Scheming stones? Don't go near
them, Mort! *Stay away!*"
Vita looked at Mort. "Is he for real?" she laughed.
"I think his misunderstandings are
very sweet," Genia sighed, curling
a lock of hair round her finger.

Mort, Weed, Genia and Vita visit the orchards...

The orchards in the centre of the island were for everyone to enjoy. Trees and bushes groaned with the weight of juicy fruits, most of which Mort and Weed didn't recognize, as growing fruit on Brutalia was a fruitless task. (They sometimes painted potatoes a cherry colour just to dream.)

"Try one of these, Weed," Genia said, pulling on a bough. Weed plucked the fruit that dangled from it. Its skin was pink and hard as leather. He looked up her, confused.

"Inside there are ruby-red seeds. Delicious. It's called a pomegranate," she explained.

"Did you just make that word up?" Mort asked because it really did sound completely bonkers.

"All words are made up, Mort," Vita giggled.

"But this was made up years ago."

"I'm glad we made up," said a misunderstanding Weed, shyly glancing at Genia.

## Mort takes a moment...

While Weed and the girls were plucking fiddly seeds from a silly-sounding pomegranate, Mort strolled out of the orchard and into a field that waved with long grasses and danced with long grasshoppers. He breathed in the sweet air and smiled, happy in the knowledge that on this earth there were places that were peaceful – like Dead Man's Island and Bonrock – and hopeful that one day Brutalia would lift itself out of the grotty bog of despair and join them.

After the montage was finished, Mort and Weed stared at the girls with something that might be mistaken for a massive crush.

"Before you fall in love with us, we have to tell you that we're not entirely happy with your behaviour. We found Vita's toucan caged on your boat." Genia frowned, and Vita narrowed her eyes in extreme disappointment.

"The horrible thing bit me!" Weed spluttered. "It's evil."

"Tickety-Boo was *scared*, Weed," Vita said. "You'd bite too, if you saw strange hands coming towards you. You've probably traumatized him now."

"Tickety-Boo?"

"Yes, Tickety-Boo was not feeling tickety-boo when we found him. And there was a raven shouting *NO MORE* – he was really, really distressed!"

"He was saying *KNOW MORE*," Mort corrected.

"Oh well, either way, we do not believe in caging animals," Genia said. "So we set him free."

# OOPS.

# CHAPTER TEN
# A WORKOUT FOR SPINDLY ARMS

*"You exercise, don't you, Ratto?"*

*"Sure do, Ratty. I do weights."*

*"Yeah, me too. I waits for
food to come my way."*

"Well, this is a fine mess!" Weed panted.

He was doing star jumps, Mort was doing sit-ups, and they were being watched over by a woman who said she wouldn't be taking any nonsense. She had a whistle resting in her lips and a badge that said:

# Arora Atlas – PE Teacher

"Isn't it a **fine** mess, Mort?" Weed insisted. "A **total** mess. An **ABSOLUTE** mess. Oh, I wish Genia was here to give me another synonym. She's clever like that, isn't she, Mort?"

Mort grunted as he endured another painful sit-up, too caught up in his own confusion, turmoil and chaos to answer. For Roger was on his way back to Brutalia, and as soon as Throt Gutsem saw that doomsday bird he'd be launching boats filled with violent Brutalians to dispatch the Bonrockians in indescribably brutal ways. But we won't go into that...

**All right, we will. But only because you asked so nicely.**

*Indescribably brutal ways an army of Brutalians would use to dispatch an enemy include: stabbing, jabbing, poking and prodding. Slicing, ripping, cutting and cleaving. Lopping, chopping, hacking and axing. And a quick kicking of the shins for good measure.*

**Satisfied?**

It might have taken ten hours to navigate the rickety *Snorty Nancy* through the Salty Sea's dangerous whirlpools and currents, but as the crow flies it was only two hours between Brutalia and Bonrock. And so – as ravens are related to crows – within a day, there would be bloodshed.

Of course, when Genia had mentioned Roger's release, Mort had spilled the beans – because honesty is the best policy – and the two girls didn't like those beans one bit.

```
            Vita:
YOU are members of the Brutalian
Army?

            Weed:
I don't know why you told them
that bit, Mort.

            Mort:
Honesty is the best policy.

            Weed:
I'm not sure it is actually.
```

Genia:
I am so disappointed in you.

Mort:
Maybe you're right, Weed.

Vita:
So you're telling us that an army
is on its way to slaughter every
single one of us? Why?

Weed:
Because you're strangers.

Genia:
I think you'll find that YOU are
the strangers here.

Mort:
This is just a matter of
geography. (Come to think of
it, that's really deep and
meaningful.)

Vita:
Perfect! We'll just explain that
to this nasty Battle-Chief of
yours, and everything will be
fine.

Mort:
I don't think that's going to be
enough. Throt has been looking
forward to a really good war.
It's going to be hard to talk him
out of it.

Vita:
Then we're doomed.

Weed:
Don't you have an army?

> Genia:
> We're pacifists, you ignoramus.
> And we thought you were too.
>
> Vita:
> This doesn't look good, boys.

Weed had been devastated at being called an ignoramus by the girl he'd secretly decided he wanted to marry one day, when they were all grown up and ready for that sort of thing. But more devastating was the way Genia and Vita looked. They had once been so happy and bright – as if they were made of sunbeams and glitter. Now they were stooped and miserable, like Brutalians on the happiest day of their lives.

Without another word, they had turned away, and a minute later Arora Atlas, flanked by some of the Bonrock Gymnastics Team, had escorted Mort and Weed back to the hostel and locked them in. And that is how Mort and Weed found themselves enduring a workout routine in the lead-up to war. Things really couldn't get any worse.

### "Press-ups – one hundred. Now!"

Things just got a little worse.

Arora Atlas fell forward on to her hands and sprang

into a few demonstration push-ups that she made look easy-peasy. Weed and Mort reluctantly lay on their bellies and tried to heave their bodies off the floor using their arms, and quickly discovered that it wasn't in the slightest bit easy-peasy. It was hardy-wardy.

"Curse my spindly arms!" Weed cried.

"If we weren't about to die horribly," Arora said, standing over them, "I would be writing you a personalized exercise plan to get you into shape."

"I don't think our bodies are made for exercise," Weed groaned.

"Of course they are!" Arora laughed with a hearty boom. "Your muscles just need to be shocked into action, coaxed like ferrets and tickled like eels. Give me a hundred more, boy."

"I can't," Mort said.

"You can." She squatted beside Mort and patted him on the back. "It's all in the mind, son – strength, fear, bravery, endurance. It's right up here in your noggin! The power of the mind is a great motivator and a terrific weapon. Mind over matter. You just need to believe."

Mort nodded and sniffed back a sob. Even facing impending doom, which was totally Mort and Weed's fault, this nice PE teacher was offering words of motivation and strategies for getting fit.

And that's when it hit him like one of his mother's well-aimed soup spoons.

## KADONK!

Mort sat up, with words dancing round his head – words that had meaning (which is most of them, even tomato). And he drifted into a dream state where the words did press-ups and star jumps and jiggled around as if they were warming up for a race.

**"Are you all right there, son?"**

"Mort, what's the matter?"

**"He's probably overdone it a bit. Are you seeing stars?"**

"Mort, it's Weed. I'm right here. Talk to me!"

**"Go and fetch some water!"**

"Who, me?"

**"No, I was talking to one of the incredible physical specimens of the Bonrock Gymnastics Team standing guard outside the door."**

While they were trying to work out what was wrong, Mort was lining up his words in a row, ready for the 100-metre sprint to the finish line. It was a race of **BRILLIANT IDEAS**.

Of all the words that raced, these were the first ones to cross the line:

**SHOCKED INTO ACTION**

**THE POWER OF THE MIND
IS A TERRIFIC WEAPON**

**YOU JUST NEED TO BELIEVE**

**MIND OVER MATTER**

**WINNING STRATEGY**

**TOMATO**

**MOTIVATION**

**HUMAN HEART**

ON YOUR MARKS, GET SET ...

**WHOOOOOSH!**

A member of the gymnastics team threw a bucket of water at Mort's head just as he shouted:

# "EUREKA!"

"That means *I've got it*," Weed said confidently, looking at the others in the room. "It's got nothing to do with reeking."

The Bonrockian gymnasts already knew that, but they nodded politely as Weed was clearly proud of this nugget of knowledge that he'd picked up on a previous adventure.

"Er ... *what* have you got, Mort?"

"A plan. A plan that could save Bonrock."

"We're listening," said all those who were listening. Those who weren't, weren't.

"Well, Weed and me—"

"Weed and I," Genia corrected.

"Technically and grammatically, you are correct, Genia," Vita agreed. "But we understand what he means, and that's all that matters when our time is running out. Go on, Mort."

"Um, Weed and I must leave right now. That means you'll have to free us."

"Perfect sentence structure," Genia said and clapped her hands.

"And then what?" Vita said. "*And what then?* Which sounds better? I can't decide."

**"I don't like the sound of any of it!"**

The thin, gravelly voice came from the small lungs of a tiny man who had shuffled his way through the crowd of gymnasts and clever girls to stare at the Brutalian warmongers.

"Mort, Weed, this is our leader, Beast," said Vita.

There followed the kind of silence that only people

who have felt simultaneously awkward, embarrassed and confused might recognize. In Mort and Weed's world, a beast was big and gruff and likely to crush your spirit and bones with a cruel *mwah-ha-ha!* This man was more of a wee beastie, like a mouse.

"*He has a giant mind,*" Genia whispered by way of explanation.

Beast circled the boys. "So you have a plan that can fix this current problem?" he asked.

"Don't ask me," Weed said. "Mort doesn't tell me anything."

Beast raised an eyebrow. "So you keep secrets from each other?"

"No," Mort said. "I've only just thought of it, and I haven't yet had the chance to tell *anyone.*"

"But you're certain it works, this plan of yours?"

"I can't be absolutely certain, obviously. I'd be lying if I said I was."

Mort's plan was ambitious, daring and not entirely sensible. He wanted to be honest about that.

"And it involves setting you free?"

"Yes, it does."

"And why should we believe you?"

Genia stepped forward. "Beast, I think they are incapable of lying. They tell the truth even when it makes them look a bit silly. And, when I say a bit silly, I mean REALLY silly. And they didn't have to tell us about the raven, remember? It seems to me that although Brutalia is a violent realm its people are honest. I trust them one hundred per cent."

"Me too," said Vita.

Weed looked at Mort in a way that said, *What just happened?*

Mort looked at Weed in a way that said, *Told you – honesty is the best policy.*

Beast nodded. "All right, then. To the din-din room! We shall discuss tactics as we feast on the hearts of human men."

*WHAT?* The boys fell to their knees.

**"WE'VE BEEN TRICKED!"** Weed wailed.

Beast picked them up by their scruff of their tunics and chuckled. "You're right, girls. Brutalians don't get jokes."

## CHAPTER ELEVEN
# THE LOOMING KEBAB

*"Ahoy, me hearties. Let's be pirates."*

*"You make me a pie, and I'll
rate it out of ten."*

*"One more terrible joke like that and
I'll make you walk the plank, Ratty."*

Mort and Weed were back aboard the *Snorty Nancy* and bracing themselves for what was to come. In the distance, Brutalia's Mists of Despair were skulking on the skyline, and directly ahead of them was the unmarked border between the two oceans, where Bonrock's sweet-natured waters were being attacked by the Salty Sea. The thundering waters spat and tugged at the tropical ocean like a hair-pulling bully with crab-claw fists. Seabirds scattered in fright as sharky behemoths snapped at their feet, and pretty fish darted in panic as salty swordfish advanced, looking for something colourful to kebab.

Mort stared glumly at the churning turmoil. It was a just small sea-based version of what would happen if his plan didn't work. There would be tugging, smashing, snapping... And kebabbing.

## PAPAAAAARP-PFFFFT...

The sound of a royal horn being suffocated by fog limped through the air and hit Mort and Weed in the ears like a rancid airborne sock.

"Get ready," Mort said, passing Weed a flask. "Remember: sow the seeds of fear."

"Sow the seeds of fear. Right." Weed swigged from the flask.

"Not in your mouth – down your front!"

"But it's so yummy."

"I agree with you, Weed. These tomato things are ridiculously delicious. But we need to focus on what's up ahead."

And what was in front of them was the *Golden Behind*, which sounds more confusing than it is. Poking through the swirling vapour, the mast of the Queen's ship appeared, and at the top its proud insignia, the **Cabbage and Crossbow**, slapped the sky.

---

*(Here's a little space where you can draw it. Hint: it's just a cabbage and a crossbow).*

---

The crossbow represented **FIGHT** and the cabbage represented **STINK**, and Throt Gutsem was coming, intent on a **STINKING FIGHT**. Obviously.

The ship's prow then broke through the Mists of Despair, its planks and steel groaning with rust and disgust, its sailors puking over the sides. But not Throt. He was standing at the helm in the position he'd like his victor's statue to be carved in (he thought of these things) – legs apart and hands on hips, steely gaze fixed on the horizon. And, although Mort couldn't see from this distance, he knew the man's eyes were gleaming in anticipation, like wet clams with fists full of lottery tickets.

Throt's war game was about to begin. Could Mort and Weed outmanoeuvre him?

"Weed, look desperate in three ... two ... one ... **NOW!**"

The boys began waving for attention, yelling as loudly as they could to stop the *Golden Behind* from going in front, which, again, is less confusing than it sounds.

**"STOP! STOP!"**

They screamed until their throats were sore. But the noise on board – the heave-hoing as the crew pulled the ropes and the oars – meant they couldn't be heard. And, on top of the grunts and groans, there was Throt Gutsem's team talk, which he delivered in a long stream with no punctuation. It was about fighting for your country and feeling the weight of responsibility for future generations and proving yourself as a citizen and can't you feel the victory in your nostrils and the power in your armpits and the thrill of the fight and all that ... etc. ... etc....

Eventually, he had to take a breath, and that's when Mort changed tack. Instead of shouting, **"STOP!"**, he shouted:

# "Atteeeeeention!"

Remarkably, like well-trained lobsters, the crew of the *Golden Behind* stopped what they were doing and stood to attention, including the anchor boy, who dropped his rope. So, rather fortuitously, the anchor plummeted down into the water and the ship shuddered to a standstill. Someone who was vomiting over the side spotted Mort and Weed, and rope ladders were thrown down for them to board.

Mort and Weed tethered the *Snorty Nancy* to the back of the *Golden Behind* and then clambered up the ladders, their hearts a-galloping like Bonrock stallions, but full of fear, like kittens entering a Grot Bear's cage.*

Throt was standing centre-deck, and behind him was the army – a motley crew of Brutalians he'd amassed in haste. "I give the orders around here!" he thundered. **"Atteeeeeention!"**

Mort and Weed did the standing-to-attention thing as Throt looked them up and down, his eyes widening at the sight of the ruby-red splats on their fronts.

Doris the Great, who had been promoted to one

---

*No kittens were harmed in the making of this simile.

of the army's highest ranks (she had formerly been a weaver and gone by the name Doris the Basket), pointed and gasped.

"What's that? Rat juice?" she said. "They got free rats on that island, boy?"

"It's not food. It's..." Mort waited until they were all ears (even though some of them had none after a nasty punishment). "It's **BLOOD**."

"Have you started the battle without me?" Throt roared. "You were to wait for my command before you began dispatching those scheming strangers!"

"It's not Bonrockian blood, sir," Mort said, standing at ease and then snapping to attention again, to look extra army-like. "It's the blood of their prisoners. We were forced to watch them being tortured."*

Throt's Adam's apple did a little jig, and his neck veins pulsed below his skin like electrified shoelaces. He paced the deck, each footstep thudding like the beat of a doom drum.

Mort thought he detected fear in the great warrior. Maybe Throt wasn't the courageous Battle-Chief he

---

*At this point, Mort thought that, seriously, honesty could take a break.

pretended to be. Perhaps he was a coward. If so, part two of the plan wouldn't be required. Mort really hoped that was the case because it was a bit of a stretch, even by Mort the Meek standards.

Throt spun round. "I'm afraid—" he said (which sounded promising). "I'm afraid there won't be time to run through tactics again, crew. The time to attack is now. And personally I can't wait."

*Oh, double rats.* He wasn't a coward. That meant that everything hinged on part two being a success. But Mort hadn't even finished part one yet, and, as you know if there's pudding on offer, you can't have seconds without finishing your firsts.

"Before we attack, we must brief you," Mort said.

"You want me to debrief you?" Throt asked.

"I'd like to keep my pants on if you don't mind," said Weed, who had got his briefs* muddled up.

"Yes, brief, debrief, whatever you like," Mort said hurriedly. "Because there are things you need to know

---

*BRIEF is a homophone that's also a homonym
– a word that sounds AND is spelled the same, but means
something different. They can be extra tricky. Just ask a
police detective on holiday if he's investigating any cases.

before you attack. Intelligence," he added, tapping his nose and wondering why he didn't tap his head, where most brains are located.

"All right, then, but keep it brief," Throt said, tossing yet another meaning of brief on to the bonfire of briefs.

"They don't just kill their prisoners... They **rip their hearts out**."

**"YURGH!"** said Doris the Great.

"What do you mean, *yurgh*?" Throt barked. "No high-ranking officer of the Brutalian Army should be so easily revolted. You're demoted."

"To Doris the Not-so-Great?"

"To Doris the Average." Throt turned back to Mort. "Now, you were saying?"

Mort panicked. This was supposed to be shocking, not an invitation to discuss ranking. He shouted, "Yes! **THEY RIP HEARTS OUT!!!**"

"They **EAT** them too," Weed added, winking at Mort.

Mort winked back. Excellent improvisation! He ran with it.

124

"And they're looking for a new supply. If we take this ship into Bonrock's harbour, we'll be heartless."

"Sounds terrific," Throt said, breathing in deeply and dreaming of statues. "Throt the Heartless."

"No," Mort persisted. "Heartless, as in you'll have no heart. It'll be removed from your chest cavity, and you'll die."

There was a moment of stillness, and Mort prayed that Throt was thinking he might prefer to keep his heart inside his chest cavity. But then the Battle-Chief's mouth twitched.

"This is hilarious! Ha ha! What a splendid joke. You boys know what I like, don't you! So let's sail on and take Bonrock down."

"B – but—" Weed said, pointing at his splattered top.

Throt sneered. "Eating rat delicately isn't the easiest of feats, so in future, if you can't handle rat politely, then don't handle it at all. This army should be a slick, clean fighting machine."

The army behind him, who looked more like a rabble of rotten sardines, shuffled awkwardly.

**"ACTION STATIONS!"** Throt roared and, as

they scuttled back to their oars and ropes, he struck up a song – a song that the crew had learned by heart, knowing they had to sing the lines in italic.

**"I don't know but it's been said,**

*I don't know but it's been said,*

**Throt Gutsem will kill 'em dead.**

*Throt Gutsem will kill 'em dead.*

**Am I right or wrong?**

*You're right.*

**Am I going strong?**

*Let's fight.*

**Brutalia!**

*Hell, yeah!*

**Brutalia!**

*Smells, yeah!*

**Brutalia's the place where we belong.**

*Let's sing it again!*

**I don't know but it's been said,**

*I don't know but it's been said..."*

etc.

As the boat skittered into the calm waters of the tropical ocean, Mort looked at the people around him aboard the *Golden Behind*. And suddenly his worry wasn't whether the plan would work, but whether the Bonrockians would take one look at this boat of rude and revolting people with pointy sticks and murderous intentions and decide that the world would be better off without them.

# CHAPTER TWELVE
# THE SPLAT ATTACK

*"Are you scared of new people
and places, Ratto?"*

*"Not at all. I'm sure the Bonrock colony
will give us a big, warm welcome."*

*"Sounds like a furry-tail story, Ratto."*

"Ooh, isn't it pretty!" said Doris the Average, pointing at Bonrock harbour, where flags with *Welcome Brutalia* were rippling in the breeze. A welcome party of toucans flapped their way towards the *Golden Behind*.

"It's not pretty – it's a trap. They're trying to make us feel welcome. You're demoted again."

"To Doris the Disappointing?"

"Doris the Blob."

"Oh."

"Too late for pitiful vowels now. There's no alternative: we have to attack with brutal force."

"There is an alternative. We can go home," Mort said. But his words were washed away on the flying spittle of Throt's command.

**"READY, EVERYONE!"** Throt thrust a crossbow into Mort's hands. "You can take the first shot, boy."

"Me? Why me?"

"As a reward for your commitment and bravery, and for making me laugh. Heartless! That's the best joke I've heard in ages. Saying one thing but meaning another. Took me by surprise. Genius."

As Mort's hand closed round the weapon, he thought *oh dear* very loudly in his head. Because Throt's words had triggered a worry. *Saying one thing but meaning another. Took me by surprise.*

He looked down at the crossbow in his hands. He had told Vita and Genia that he was a pacifist, so what would they think if they saw him holding one of the most lethal weapons known to human-kind? What if they thought he was double-crossing them? What if they suddenly believed he'd tricked them, and that part two of his plan was to actually attack them?

Or wait...

What if they'd tricked **HIM**?

What if they *were* luring the *Golden Behind* into a trap?

What if they *were* armed with things that could make you dead?

What if their bright birds *weren't* carrying croaks of merry welcome but things that might explode and send the Brutalians to the bottom of the tropical sea with a tickety-BOOM!

His brain loaded with what-ifs and the fear of a toucan missile crisis, Mort began to panic.

Weed saw that he was struggling. "What's the matter, Mort? Your knuckles are going white. Are you scared or do you just really love holding that crossbow tightly? Because, if it's that, then I think we need to revisit the Pacifist Promise. Really quietly, though, because if Throt hears us he'll probably say we're killing morale. Then he'll probably kill us to boost it again."

Mort mumbled along:

**"I, a member of the Pacifist Society of Brutalia, promise not to hurt anything."**

"Mort, you usually say it with such gusto, and I'm sorry to tell you, but that sounded limper than a squid's salute."

Mort looked at his friend, for whom everything was so simple. Bluffing and war games and tactics and deceit probably hadn't even crossed his sweet little mind.

*You only know what you know.*

And the only thing Mort knew at this very moment was that he was a non-cheating, honest pacifist. Sometimes just sticking to what you knew and hoping others would see what was in your heart (without taking it out to look at it) was the only thing you could do. Especially when the rest was out of your hands.

Throt paced the decks. "They're already waiting for us, so that's the element of surprise gone. We'll have to go straight to my next tactic – intimidation. Get ready to roar."

The Battle-Chief began prodding everyone with his little cane, riling them up, getting them angsty and ants-in-their-pantsy, so when the time came they could release the roar and scare the briefs off those Bonrockians.

The *Golden Behind* sped across the calm waters, and as the seconds ticked down Throt bristled with the promise of some bloody* action.

Mort bent down and placed the crossbow on the floor.

"What are you DOING?" Throt bellowed.

---

*This is not swearing – bloody means 'with lots of blood'.

"Tying my shoelaces," Mort said.

Which wasn't a lie because he had quickly untied them first. But when he stood up he was holding no weapon – just a head full of hope that part two would go as planned, and that they weren't about to be murdered by smiling Bonrockians or blown up by war toucans.

Just then, a flock of the crazy-beaked birds flew above them in formation, like rainbow-tipped spears.

Mort held his breath as they passed over. Not a single one of them exploded.

One did, however, do a massive plop on Throt's shoulder, which he took as a declaration of war.

"ADVANCE!" he yelled. "And ROAR!"

As the sails picked up the breeze and the rowers picked up the pace, Throt picked up his pep talk, only this time it wasn't about the thrill of victory – he was filling them with fears and threats, so the people in his army felt they had everything to lose if they didn't fight to the death.

"Let's kill them to save your children and keep Brutalia safe! Death to Bonrock!"

The ship raced into the harbour, with its ragamuffin

army of Brutalians roaring their lungs up – and you could see by their reddened, spittle-flecked faces that it made them feel a bit powerful. Too powerful perhaps. Stupidly powerful. Throt's aggression was contagious, and if they all started to feel as invincible as him then the plan would fall flatter than Weed's press-ups.

Mort grabbed his friend. "We need to say something as an antidote to Throt's poisonous pep talk. Quickly – spread the story of the hearts again. We need them to believe the Bonrockians are ruthless."

In the time that remained before they reached the docks, Mort and Weed wove through the soldiers, whispering of what they'd seen: bobbing red hearts in great soup pans, chefs' hands covered in gore as they sliced them up (with added details like squish, splurge, squidge and squelch). And then they sowed their (fruit) seeds of fear.

"You won't be much good to your country if your heart's on a plate."

"If you die, you'll never fight again."

By the time the boat's nose touched the harbour wall, the army's cry was more of a wibble.

Throt surged like a bull to the front of the boat. "Bonrockians, prepare to—"

Something hit him in the face, stopping him abruptly.

**"H-h-heart!"** shrieked Doris the Blob, who didn't care about sounding cowardly because in terms of demotion there was nowhere else to go.

There was a silence that fizzed with tension. Throt stared at the red splodge that was now sliding down the front of his breastplate. A dripping mush of a human heart.

"So it wasn't a joke?" he hissed.

"No, funnily enough," Mort replied.

"Good. Even more reason to **FIIIIIIGGGGGGGGGGHHT!**"

Throt's cry of **FIIIIIIGGGGGGGGGGHHT** (with seven i's) was supposed to be the cue for the Brutalian Army to leap off the *Golden Behind* and attack, but even the most brutal of the brutes stopped at the sight of Bonrockians loading their bows with heart-tipped arrows. The red balls gleamed in the light, all shiny and oozy and coronary.

Beast, who was on the shoulders of Arora Atlas so he could be seen, gave his command:

"LET 'EM FLY, ME HEARTIES!"

Before you could say **tivver me shimbers**, the *Golden Behind* was pelted with a rain of cold, slippery redness.

Weeeeee SPLURGE

EVERYBODY FREAK OUT!

zZZZZzZzZZZZZYUCK!

ssSSSSssSsSSPlat

humumumanumaHEART

Hearts fell on the heads of the Brutalians, who, instead of launching a counterattack with weapons that could actually do some damage, dropped their crossbows, spears and rocks. They skidded on the skins and the juices of the strange fruitables as they hastily hoisted the sails and manned the ropes.

"It's only a few vital organs!" Throt screamed, but the veins in his neck were the only things standing to attention.

The illusion of invincibility was broken. Fear had set in. The Brutalian Army was armless, harmless and now looking like a boat filled with contestants from a horrible game show called **I'm a Brutalian, Get Me Outta Here!** And no amount of roaring from Throt made any difference. The crew weighed anchor, put the *Golden Behind* into reverse and backed away from Bonrock Island.

Mort and Weed stood in the shower of tomatoes, trying not to smile.

"*Well, that's that!*" whispered Weed. "*Job well done. Thank goodness peace is restored.*"

"I wouldn't be so sure," Mort said.

They looked through the cabin window at Throt, who had unrolled a piece of parchment on the captain's table and was now drawing attack plans with arrows and stick people and words like **GET 'EM** and **GUT 'EM**.

"Genia wouldn't be very pleased with his spelling," Weed tutted, adding a lovestruck sigh.

"But Vita would say that he's communicated well enough," Mort said. "And what it's telling me is that the battle might be over today, but the war has just begun. Unless we find a way to create lasting peace, then this won't be the last time the *Golden Behind* creates a stink."

As the ship sailed out of calm waters, the Salty Sea came at them with full force. Huge waves threw themselves at the vessel and crashed on to the deck. As it rocked from side to side, sailors, tomatoes and seawater sloshed about like a vicious nautical soup.

*A vicious soup*, Mort said to himself. And the whisper of a plan brushed his brain, before a tumbling barrel dislodged by the storm knocked him out cold.

# CHAPTER THIRTEEN
# SLIME IS SYMBOLIC OF NOTHING

*"Hooray, the war is over!"*

*"But there will be more
offensives to come, Ratty."*

*"Offensive what? Smells, words, gestures?"*

*"Knowing this writer –
all of the above."*

When Mort opened his eyes, it was dawn, and Brutalia's silhouette sat like a large burnt cake on the naer horizon. They were home. But not home and dry because, even by the dim light of the early sun, Mort could see that Throt was soggy and furious.

The warrior no longer looked like a bionic superhero. His muscles drooped like a waxwork next to a radiator, his hair was scruffy, and Mort could see a small hermit crab hiding in the cleft of his chin. Throt hadn't expected to be hit by a huge, salty, creature-filled wave as he came out on deck, and he hadn't intended to lose his precious war. This dire combination made him crabby in every way possible.

"You boys are a disgrace," he spat. "You sent the raven signal telling me that Bonrock was vulnerable and ready for us to attack. And what did I find? The entire island prepared for our arrival!"

"Letting Roger go was a mistake," Mort said. "That's the truth."

"And we did try to warn you about the hearts," mumbled Weed.

"You told me that was a joke!" Throt roared.

"No, that's what *you* said," Weed corrected.

"I know what I heard. You definitely said it was a joke. And I know one person who won't be laughing and that's the Queen!"

Throt's veins and muscles did a bit more twitching and trembling before he spun about to give orders for docking. He spun back again. "You boys go back to your boat and don't come ashore until it's clean. I want it spick and span, top to bottom, shined up nice until I can see the *Golden Behind* in its reflection."

"Wood doesn't reflect no matter how hard you polish it," Weed said, but luckily Throt had marched off.

With a gaslight in their hands, they climbed down the rope ladder and back aboard the *Snorty Nancy*, which had been bucking in the wake of the *Golden Behind* all the way home. It was covered in all manner of the Salty Sea's spew, and most of it was in the cabin, which now appeared to be home to four octopuses, nine lobsters and a whole herd of carnivorous clams.

"We'd better start by bailing out the water," Mort suggested, prising a clam from his elbow.

He grabbed a bucket and began to fling squidgy squiddy things overboard. Most of them crawled right back in again because they were badly behaved. The boys toiled for hours, making very little progress with unhousing the watery animals, which were attracting greedy seabirds.

One particularly large, feathered beast landed with a thud on Mort's head.

"Mort. Don't be alarmed, but there's a toucan on your bonce."

The toucan very carefully stepped down Mort's face and on to his shoulder, where it turned to face him, looking Mort directly in the eye.

Mort froze, and so would you if a beak the size of ten generous noses was pressed up against yours. When his eyes managed to focus, he saw that along the beak were written the words

*Come back soon! Don't be a stranger! V&G*

The bird then launched itself from Mort's head, flapped out through the cabin door and sailed the air currents back to Bonrock, careful to stay high above the snapping waves.

"That was nice," Weed said.

"Yes, but..."

"But what?"

"Nothing, Weed. I thought I had an idea, but it's gone."

"Oh well, I'm sure it'll come back. We'd better get this boat impossibly shiny."

As the boat was towed into the docks, the boys continued to scrub the decks furiously. But Weed was right – wood isn't reflective – and seeing as Throt had stationed guards on the boardwalks to prevent them coming ashore, it looked as if they'd never get off the *Snorty Nancy*.

The boys were getting nowhere fast (which makes absolutely no sense).

"Ahoy there!"

"Ngoshi?" Mort and Weed sloshed to the back of their grotty boat to see the sea-faring trader girl sailing nearby.

"What are you doing here, so close to Brutalia?" Mort asked.

"Just checking out where you live. I like to visit my

friends from time to time – to see if there's a trade to be done."

"I wouldn't visit this place," Weed said. "Not if you want to keep those pretty earlobes."

Ngoshi giggled. "You're so funny."

"We're serious actually," Mort said. "And anyway we don't have anything worth trading here."

"There's always something." Ngoshi thought for a while. "For instance, if you have any more clams, I could give you a couple of gunge corals. Nothing cleans and gleams quite as good as a gunge coral!"

She winked a twinkly eye, and Mort and Weed's jaws dropped open like trapdoors.

"You're good at this!" Weed said.

"That's because I love my job," Ngoshi said. "There's always something people need and, with trading, everyone's a winner. So is it a deal?" She held up her little hand for them to shake.

Within minutes, Ngoshi had sailed away with a happy, "See ya!" and a small bag of clams, and Mort and Weed were back to scrubbing the decks of the *Snorty Nancy*.

With the clear slime that oozed from the corals, the planks soon began to gleam, not only reflecting their faces, but also the *Golden Behind* (which was just in front).

"We're doing it, Mort!" Weed said, leaping about. "It's shining up proper, nice as pie."

They coated the boat from top to bottom, covering the *Snorty Nancy* in a thick layer of goo. On close inspection, you could see that it wasn't a hard shine but a slathering of gloopy ooze. However, the guards didn't inspect it closely – they were getting hassled by aggressive crablets and wanted to go home. Mort and Weed were free to leave.

As they made their way up the hill from the docks, something tickled Mort's brain. "Do you reckon the slime is symbolic, Weed? I can't help thinking it means something."

"Slime waits for no one?" Weed said, nodding back towards the boat.

The squeezed-out corals they'd left on deck had begun soaking up all the gunge they'd only just splurged out, and the *Snorty Nancy* was quickly transforming back into a blistered old wreck that looked as if it had a bad cold.

Mort shrugged. "You're right. Slime is symbolic of nothing."

Mort's brief jubilation disappeared along with the gunk as he was hit with a large sponge of wet helplessness. Plan one and plan two had gone according to plan, but the boys had nothing up their sleeves for what should come next. And what would be coming next wasn't going to be pretty. Throt was certain to attack Bonrock again – it was clear from the roll of parchment on his desk, which said WHEN I ATTACK BONROCK AGAIN, and it was also written all over the Battle-Chief's face.

Mort couldn't forget it – blotches of white and purple mottled every part of the man's skin. He was like a human boil, threatening to explode.

And OOPS! That human boil was waiting for Mort at the top of the hill.

But he was no longer looking as if he might explode. Instead, Throt Gutsem looked as if all the bad stuff that had been bursting to come out was now poisoning his insides, like sarcastic pufferfish.

He grabbed Mort's neck in his large hard. "I'm taking you to see the Queen," he growled.

"Why?" Mort gasped through his restricted larynx.

"For sabotaging the mission. You're a spy. Snit Parlot heard you say so!"

"I never said I was a spy!"

Weed tugged at Throt's arm. "It was me. I said 'nice as pie'."

But it didn't matter what was or wasn't said. Throt wanted someone to blame, and the Queen probably wanted someone to pain. It was a match made in hell.

"Mort Canal. Otherwise known as Mort the Meek, Your Majesty," Marcus Sucram boomed.

Mort was **thrown** to the floor in the **throne** room, for no other reason than Marcus Sucram got his homophones muddled up.

The Queen and King were sitting on their plush velvet chairs inside a giant glass bubble, which they thought would give them extra protection against invaders. But the extra protection, while keeping things out, was also keeping things in. A fug had built up on the glass and, when the Queen wiped away a patch of condensation, her face was a picture – if the picture was of someone who was struggling with enclosed spaces.

"Ah yes, Mort the Meek. It's **ALWAYS** Mort the Meek!" she spat. "Why oh why is it always you?"

"Is that a rhetorical question?" Mort asked carefully.

"A wet oracle question? No, of course not! Only Sally McRoot answers wet oracle* questions."

Mort decided not to inform the Queen that a rhetorical question was either one that couldn't be answered, or one that everyone already knew the answer to. And a wet oracle? It just meant that she was still believing in the dubious prophecies of soup. He wondered what Sally had been saying while they were gone, to keep her position as Royal Soup Sayer.

"While you've been gone, our Royal Soup Sayer has been seeing danger in her pot – just in case you were wondering," the Queen said. "Stranger danger. Which you've only gone and made worse. Throt told me everything. Mort the Meek? Mort the *Sneak* more like. And if you've come asking for forgiveness you can forget it."

"I can explain," said Mort.

"I don't listen to the explanations of traitors. I listen only to the soup. You will be punished!"

"Plunged in a hot bog with added ingredients?" Mort gulped, unsure as to whether he did want to know or definitely did not want to know.

---

*Oracle means prophecy – handy, eh?

"That was an old punishment, you fool. The new one is **Cross the Courtyard of Doom!**"

"I think I crossed it on the way here," Mort said.

At that, the King chuckled, which blew the Queen's top. If looks could kill, Mort would be on a boat to Dead Man's Island.

"Prepare the courtyard!" the Queen yelled. "When it's ready, Mort the Meek, you will be sent for. And there'll be no getting round it with your cunning plans this time."

She threw her head back to let out a laugh, but the pigeon-feather fascinator in her hair tickled the King's nose, and he sneezed. **ACHOO. Splurge.**

"I'll get you, Mort the Meek!"

# CHAPTER FOURTEEN
# SING A SONG OF DEATH TO 'DEATH'

*"Did you know that punk rock music
originated here in Brutalia?"*

*"Um ... it's certainly an acquired taste."*

*"I think you'll find it requires no
taste whatsoever. Heh-heh-heh."*

The Queen told Marcus that Mort should be thrown out of the palace, and so he was carried out on a golden chair.

"Wow, things must have gone well," Weed said delightedly.

"No, that's Marcus Sucram getting his homophones muddled again. The truth is, I'm in a lot of trouble. She's preparing some kind of punishment for me."

"What?"

"The Courtyard of Doom. I have no idea what's going to happen, but I think it'll be bad. But my punishment is the least of our problems. We still have to save Bonrock, and I've got no idea how to do it."

"You'll think of something, Mort. You always do. In the meantime, why don't we go and visit Punky? Seeing her will remind us how we can change people's behaviour when we put our minds to it. It might inspire us with the Bonrock problem."

"You're right. If we can find a happy ending for an angry rock-crusher and a terrifying sea monster, then we can find a happy ending for any situation," Mort said.

"That's beautifully optimistic," Weed said, patting his friend on the back. "Come on. Let's see if there's a one-in-a-million chance you're right."

Mort nodded. "Yeah, all right, Weed. But don't mention my impending punishment to Punky. If she gets upset, she might go back to crushing rocks with her bare hands."

They followed the narrow track across the clifftops to the place now known as Punk Rock, where Punky Mason sat all day long, looking out over the sea for a sign of her monster friend, the giant Belgo.

When they arrived, she was standing on her rock, and below her a small crowd had gathered, hair spiked with slime, eyes circled with coal dust, just like her. She was giving a concert and, as she yelled at the top of her lungs, her fans bashed their heads against imaginary walls and screamed in each other's faces.

"It's a bit weird," Weed said as they approached. "Pretending to be angry at one another."

"Better out than in," Mort said, remembering how Punky had once been so full of rage it burst out of her like spikes.

That was before she'd discovered her love for animals and for making harmless, tuneless music. Well, perhaps not harmless – it had the power to make your ears bleed – but still, there was a hundred per cent less chance of death.

"**DEATH DEATH DEATH!**" came a cheer from the mosh pit.

"That's one of my favourite songs," Weed said.

"You're a pacifist, Weed!" Mort said. "They're saying DEATH!"

"No, listen closely. They're saying DEATH *to* DEATH. It's the opposite of death, Mort. It's just a convoluted way of saying LIFE."

Mort froze. "Say that again."

"Convoluted. I learned it from Genia. It means long-winded or complicated."

"No, the other bit."

"Death to Death?"

"No, never mind."

Mort couldn't remember exactly what his brain had latched on to, but it was something about listening... It was just a whisper of an idea, tickling like a sweet butterfly before being blown clean away by the chorus.

# "DEATH TO DEATH SET LIGHT TO THE BREATH OF YOUR INNER DEMON WAAAAAAAA! KERANG!"

"It's really quite jolly," Weed said, tapping his foot.

Then something caught Mort's eye. A figure dancing in the throng – small, wearing slate-grey rags, with hair and eyes the colour of rain clouds.

"ONO!" Mort cried. "Weed, it's Ono!"

**"DEATH TO DEATH!"** they sang, as they ran towards Punky's rockers.

After **'Death to Death'** had been sung three times (because it was everyone's favourite), the rockers left, wearing big smiles on the inside – not the outside because it didn't suit their image.

Then Mort, Weed, Punky and Ono were alone, and finally all four members of the Pacifist Society of Brutalia were together in one place. The first thing Punky did was to show them her latest tattoo. It was their new sign for peace – a circle the size of a limpet shell, with three lines inside to represent the head and three arms of the Belgo.

After that, they said the Pacifist Promise three times (because it turns out it was their favourite promise) and sat down to have a good old chat about peace.

Except peace seemed like a very shaky subject, and not just because of Throt, as Ono was about to explain...*

"We were called to lug Gloria Funkle. She's in Dad's boat on her way to Dead Man's Island."

"Gloria Funkle the composter? What killed her?" Weed said.

"Apparently, it was Lance Pollip," Ono said sadly.

"When we saw him, he did look determined to have a fight," Mort said.

---

*A recap of Ono Assunder, for those who don't know, because you only know what you know.
**Appearance:** grey hair, grey clothes, grey eyes
**Family:** the Assunders are Body Luggers – they are supposed to throw Brutalia's dead off the cliff into a watery grave, but they don't.
**Home:** Dead Man's Island** where they actually take the bodies and give them a ground burial, which is good for the plants.
**Why is Ono special?** She helps her friends to think in different ways.

---

**Dead Man's Island is a terrific holiday destination, and there are indeed brochures that advertise clean accommodation, sandy beaches, a lively bar that sells the best pawpaw juice, and gardens to astound and delight.
(You should go there and you CAN by reading the first Mort book.)

"Perhaps he was frustrated about something and didn't know how to get his emotions out. I know how that feels..." Punky suggested.

"You do, Punky," Mort said kindly. "But then you found a better way of expressing yourself."

"Helping kids pierce their eyebrows," Punky said. "Oh, and animal welfare."

"For him, it was squeezing something," Ono said.

Weed gasped. "You mean Gloria innocently went to the Pop-Shop for treatment and walked out dead?"

"Oh no," Mort said.

"Yes?" Ono replied.

"No, Ono. I meant **OH NO**. Poor Gloria Funkle." Mort hung his head. "This all feels connected in some unconnected way – which is just typical of these sorts of adventures. Unless we deal with the anger towards Bonrock, which is building like a boil, then I fear there's going to be an explosion of tragedies."

A warm hand stroked his back, and he looked up to see Ono's small grey eyes peering into his average-sized green ones. They were full of compassion, and they also swirled with optimism, as they always did. They told

Mort that life wasn't black and white, but full of shades and hues. They told him that there was a way out of this mess. He just had to find it.

"Sometimes it's good to start at the beginning. Why don't you tell us what happened," Ono said.

"All right, but I need something to use as markers."

Weed fumbled in his pockets and pulled out a handful of carnivorous clams, which he very quickly dropped. "Bit bitey, but will they do the trick?"

"We'll see how far we get," Mort laughed.

He positioned the clams on the ground in front of them. "This one is Brutalia. This is Bonrock. This is the *Golden Behind*. This is the *Snorty Nancy*. This is the *Pax Navi* – the girls' boat. Here's the Queen. And this is Sally McRoot. Now it all started when Weed and I spotted the *Pax Navi* bouncing on the waves at Crashbang Cove..."

"You forgot Ngoshi," Weed said, adding another clam to the scene.

"You're right, but I'm not sure she matters in our story," Mort said, although the moment the words left his mouth he wondered if that was true.

A whole explanation later, Mort had finished, and everyone's faces looked like flatfish at a funeral.

"So, you see, we're in a position now where the Queen wants to be protected, Throt wants to protect her so he can show how good he is at protecting, Sally McRoot wants to keep giving doomsday predictions as it's the only flavour she has in her life, and together they've persuaded the people of Brutalia that if the Bonrockians invade they'll lose everything."

"A lot of people are going to die if we don't do something," Punky said.

And there was nothing more that could be said after that, so they watched as, one after the other, the clams gobbled each other up, removing themselves from the fight, until there was just the queen clam, staring up at them with stalky eyes and licking her lips.

"As the only person with actual power, I think we have to persuade the Queen," Mort said, "who at this minute is sitting in a glass bubble, stewing in hate and unsavoury gases."

"I think you're getting somewhere," Ono said encouragingly. "But my father's waiting with the boat, so I have to go."

"Can't you stay a bit longer?" Mort said. "I hardly ever see you."

"You're always invited to Dead Man's Island. Don't be a stranger."

*Don't be a stranger.* Those words again! Mort chewed them over as the queen clam chewed his shoe.

*You're always invited. Don't be a stranger.*

"You OK, Mort? You look like you've eaten a bad clam," Punky said.

"Yes!" Mort said suddenly, standing up.

"Well, spit it out. Quickly!" Weed said, worrying about clam-belly, which is an illness you wouldn't wish on your best enemy, let alone your best friend.

Mort thought he meant spit out the idea. And he did, as soon as the idea feathers floated into place.

Don't be a stranger.

You know what you know.

People are scared of what they don't know.

Listen and understand.

He looked up brightly. "To stop the fighting, we need to understand WHY. WHY does the Queen want to fight?"

"Because she's a big meanie?"

"Kind of, Weed. She's mean because she's scared of losing her grip over her people. And she wants to fight because she's *terrified* of losing her country."

"But Bonrock doesn't want to take her country. It was just dodgy soup," Weed said.

"When people look for signs all the time, they'll eventually find them."

"I see... Because she's scared, she's trying to be even scarier," Punky said. "I know how that feels too."

"Yes, you do, Punky. Attack was your form of defence."

"So do we have to defend the Queen or attack her?" Weed asked.

"Neither. We have to show her that life isn't black and white."

"Shall we show her that it's white and black?"

"That's just turning things around." Mort froze. "Weed, you're a genius. And I think I've worked out how Ngoshi fits into our story!"

# CHAPTER FIFTEEN
# GETTING TO THE BOTTOM OF IT

*"Did you know I once found a
potato that looked like a rat?"*

*"Did you, Ratty? How did it look like a rat?"*

*"It had whiskers, Ratto."*

*"I think that was probably
just mould, Ratty."*

"This one's my favourite," Sally said, pressing a potato into Mort's hands. "See that? It's a crack—"

"Sally—"

"Soup Sayer."

"Sorry. Soup Sayer, we've actually come to introduce you to a new soup ingredient."

"Is it shaped like a bum?"

"Well, actually, it is a bit."

After Mort had been struck by the idea of turning things around, they had rushed back to the *Snorty Nancy* and gathered up all the fruitables that had splattered down on to the boat during Bonrock's attack. He now emptied the sack on to her table.

Sally shrieked. "What's that bloody mess?"

"It's not blood. It's FLAVOUR. Give us an hour, and we'll give you the soup of your dreams."

"Don't be ridiculous! The soup of my dreams is in my dreams, and I'm not giving you access to my dreams, no siree. Now get out. I've got predictions to make."

Sally shuffled to her pot and stirred her rotten-stinking soup (which was rotten-stinking carrot with a sprinkling of gravel) and began to read it for signs.

"Ooh, it says two boys will turn up at my door."
She swung round and pointed and Mort and Weed.
"It came true!"

She turned back to her pot and stirred once more.
"It says one boy will have eyes like large chocolate
buttons and the other will have unremarkable green
ones." She swung round again. "It's true!"

"Sally, you're just saying what you can see.
We know you can't read your soup," Weed said.

"SHHHH!" she spat, jabbing her thumb at the
window. She had a point. Snit Parlot could be lurking
anywhere.

"*This ingredient might give you new predictions*,"
Mort whispered, scooping the tomato mush towards
her across the table.

Her shoulders dropped. "Just leave me alone to
pretend in peace, will ya? I don't want any more of
you or your new ingredient. There's no decent food
on Brutalia. Even the soup knows that, don't you,
soup? What, soup? What did you say? Tell the boys
to go away?"

Sally pushed the boys in the direction of the door, then ran back to her pot as it bubbled.

"What, soup? What, soup?" She looked at them desperately. "It said something then, didn't it?"

"I don't think so," Mort said.

"It's shy because you're here. Go away."

None of this difficulty came as a surprise. In fact, Mort had been prepared for it because Sally McRoot was famously unpredictable. One minute she'd offer you soup and the next she'd say you stole it from her. One day she'd steal carrots from the market and the next day she'd steal cabbages (although that was more of a shopping list). The only thing you could count on was her devotion to funny-shaped vegetables. She would run across Brutalia stark naked if she heard news of a particularly bulbous mushroom – and often did.

So the next step was easy: Weed asked to see her collection of rude veg.

Her face lit up. Then she peered into her pot. "What, soup? You think I should show him? All right, then, I will! Come along, young man. What do you want to see first? The turnips?"

167

As Weed was introduced to the decaying, knobbly vegetables, Mort quickly took over the kitchen, scraping the tomatoes into a pan and getting to work on something that would blow Sally's mind. Or her nostrils. He smiled as he remembered her words as her life hung in the balance: *"I'd give my nostrils for an ingredient that didn't taste of mud and mould."*

Well, he didn't want her nostrils; he just wanted her cooperation.

He thought back to Coochina Sapori, the chef with huge hands who somehow created tastes that could tingle the tongue off a tarantula, and he tried to recall how she'd made that hearty soup. He boiled and reduced the tomatoes down into a thick blood-coloured liquid, adding salt, which he brushed off his seawater-encrusted tunic. The pottage became thicker and tastier, and when it was ready he gave Weed the wink.

Weed winked back and turned to Sally, who was in the middle of showing him her radishes.

"Tiny bottoms," she explained. "Rows and rows of tiny bottoms, see?"

"Yes, lovely. And I've got a game for you, Sally,"

Weed said. "Why don't you close your eyes and guess which vegetable I'm feeding you?"

"Ooh, good game," she said, nodding enthusiastically. "Go on, then."

Sally closed her eyes, and Weed placed a piece of chopped turnip in her mouth, which Sally rolled round her tongue, probing its contours for a clue.

"I know! It's a turnip!"

"Very good. Now open wide and let's try something else."

Sally opened wide, and Mort quicky stuck a spoonful of tomato soup into her gob.

"*Mrhdfrrphphphsphfff*. **WHAT** did you just put in my mouth?"

Weed looked at Mort worriedly as Sally's face began to crumple like a tissue. Her forehead crunched into her eyebrows, which squished her eyes and wrinkled her nose. It was almost as if the soup had sucked all the life out of her. But then, quite suddenly, she breathed in with a giant gasp.

## *GASP*

(bigger)

# GASP

Sally McRoot reinflated. Not only her lungs and face, but her entire body. She looked brighter too, as if the years had dropped away.

**"TASTY!"** she shouted, eyes popping. "That is **TASTY!"**

"I'm glad you said that, Sally. You see—"

"TASTY!" she shrieked.

"Yes, it's—"

## **"TASTY!"**

Mort didn't try to say anything else. There wasn't much point. Sally sprang to the soup pot and drained the lot, and when she finally emerged, splattered in red and panting like a vampire who'd run a marathon, the boys knew that their plan might just work.

"Wh-wh-what *was* that?" She ran to Mort and shook him roughly.

"A tomato."

"That's not a real word," she spat. "Give me another."

"To-may-doh?"

"Nah, I prefer the first one. What is this tomato? Where did you get it?"

Mort took Sally's hands, led her to the table and sat her down. "Sally, if we tell you, you have to promise not to tell anyone else."

"Give me a tomato and I promise not to tell." She held out her hand and wiggled her fingers.

Mort thought of Ngoshi's trading skills. "As you're our friend, we're willing to do a trade with you, Sally."

"With trading, everyone's a winner," Weed added, with a wink.

Sally looked from one to the other, hands still wiggling, itching for tomatoes. She nodded. "Trade. I want to trade."

"We can get you lots and lots of tomatoes, but you have to do something for us," Mort said.

"And they're definitely shaped like bums?"

"Well, sort of, yes."

"It's a deal."

# CHAPTER SIXTEEN
# WHAT DOES THE
# SOUP SAY?

*"It would be quite fun to be a
comedian, don't you think?"*

*"Not in Brutalia. If the Queen
didn't like one of your wisecracks,
you'd be the one in stitches."*

The leaflets were spread far and wide across the island, and those who could read delivered the message to those who couldn't, and at sundown they were all gathered in the square, wondering what flavour of prediction was going to be made.

Looby Larkspit, who was shackled to Brutus the prison guard, took some guesses.

"If it's cabbage soup, life's going to **STINK**. Get it? If it's onion soup, life's going to **STING**. Get it? If it's radish soup, you're—"

The crowd began booing. But the raucousness was broken by the royal horn-blowers.

# PA-PA PA-PA PA-PA PA-PA-PA PA-PA PA-PA PA-PAAA PAH!

The crowd fell silent and the Queen and King arrived, bowled on to the stage in their fogged-up glass bubble, tumbling about inside it like bingo balls. The Queen shrieked at the guards who held up signs saying *LOOK SOMEWHERE ELSE*.

Everyone looked somewhere else, which gave the Queen time to adjust her dress and reaffix her new moth-wing eye accessories. When she was ready, she knocked on the glass. "Now look at ME!" she screamed.

Everyone did, and the square was so quiet you could have heard a mouse dropping.

"Now look at HER!" she screamed, pointing at Sally McRoot.

A curtain was drawn back to reveal the Royal Soup Sayer standing by her cauldron. Every adult, child and mouse watched quietly as she stirred the broth with a long wooden spoon.

"Tell us, Soup Sayer! What do you see?" said the Queen, moth wings a-trembling.

Sally stirred and stirred and stirred. "What, soup?" she cried. "Reveal your wisdom."

She bent her head over her pot and disappeared into the plumes of steam. Then she straightened, looking wise and informed, with a piece of onion stuck to her eyebrow. "The soup says that the strangers are not violent. They're just afraid. They *fear* us."

Then she stopped and nodded wisely.

There was silence.

And more silence.

Sally McRoot seemed to have frozen.

"She hasn't forgotten the rest, has she?" Weed said, looking at Mort desperately.

"I hope not. I really, really hope not."

"Is that IT?" the Queen yelled.

"Um..." Sally tapped her foot and hummed for a bit. Then she looked into the soup and shrugged.

The air was as tense as string that stretched from the past, through the present and into the future.

Mort had to do something. This was their one and

only chance to turn the war around. He pulled the last of the tomatoes from his pocket, gave it a kiss for good luck and then launched it towards the stage.

It sailed over the heads of the crowd like a squashed heart in a game of offal tennis.

"If you're aiming that at Sally, it won't reach!" Weed said anxiously. "We're too far away."

"Don't panic, Weed. People are scared of what they don't know."

Just as Mort had hoped, the tomato was caught and thrown away again, like a disgusting hot potato, from one person to another, each time getting closer to the stage.

**Urgh... What the...? Yuk... Get it off me... Gross... Argh!**

# SPLAT!

It landed at Sally's feet. She eyed the tomato, and realization dawned like a snail crossing a finish line. She knocked her head with the spoon. "Oh yeah! The soup also says this..."

"Inviting the strangers

Will lift the dangers.

Call them from the cliffs

And they will bring gifts.

And they've got gemstones, apparently."

She paused. "Yeah, that's it. It's not saying anything else."

"What does that mean?" the Queen gasped, her face pressed up against the bubble.

"It means that if you get to know the strangers then they won't be strangers, and there won't be dangers. And, if you invite them here, they'll bring presents. What was it again? Oh yeah – they've got opals, pearls and rubies. Personally, I'm hoping for a sack of those tomato things."

Mort gritted his teeth. *Don't go too far, Sally*, he begged silently. *Stop right there.*

But he needn't have worried. The prophecy was like music to the ears of the paranoid Queen, who might have lost her sense of reason, but certainly not her sense of smell. Happy that she wasn't about to be attacked by scheming strangers, she took the King's crown and smashed through the glass. Stepping out, she breathed in deeply.

Then realization dawned, like a perfect soufflé. "Opals, pearls, rubies! We must throw a party for our dear friends as soon as possible," she declared. "Tomorrow! Send boats this very moment, with invitations!"

In the distance, the warning bell tolled. The Belgo was close by.

"That oversized bath toy is in our waters again," the Queen tutted. "That rules out sending boats. Argh! All right, the first person to come up with a good idea gets one wish granted."

"Lift me up, Weed," Mort said. "You never know when you might need a wish."

Wobbling on the shoulders of his friend, Mort emerged above the heads of the crowd. "It's only two hours as the crow flies!" he shouted. "Ravens are related to crows. So let's send a flock of ravens!"

"You again!" the Queen shrieked. "Yes, well, fine. You are granted one wish. Scribe Pockle – have it noted."

The ancient man – keeper of Birth Certificates and Legal Documents – scribbled on his parchment:

**One wish owed to Mort Canal**

thereby making it totally legit.

# CHAPTER SEVENTEEN
# YOUR PRESENTS ARE WELCOME ON THE ISLAND OF BRUTALIA!

*"Shall we help with the guided
tours of Brutalia?"*

*"Good idea, Ratto. You show
them the alleyways, and I'll show
them the stinking sewers."*

*"Trust you to bagsy
the best bits, Ratty!"*

The Brutalians stood on the clifftops and watched
as a dark cloud rolled across the sky towards them.
It wasn't swirling doom, like you'd expect from a story
like this – it was a flock of 368 ravens returning from
their mission. (Originally, there were 400 but 32 ended
up as swordfish kebabs.)

The chief raven had a piece of paper in its beak.

**Thanks for the invite. We're on our way.**
**Love, the people of Bonrock**

So yes, there were visitors to Brutalia after all.
A boatload of Bonrockians. They came a-bobbing
across their calm turquoise waters before a-rocking
and a-rolling through the vicious Salty Sea, and they
approached the spiky nation of Brutalia, remembering
to avoid Crashbang Cove.

They moored their ships at marginally less perilous
docks, where Throt was waiting, looking as if he'd
swallowed a sticky wasp pudding. He had been stood

down as Brutalia's Battle-Chief and was now wearing a
badge that said:

**Brutalia's Welcome
Committee
Ask me anything!**

Humiliation had caused his jaw to slacken and his
posture to sag like a disappointed sloth. There was
barely a whiff of battle left about him. And, to make
things worse, the first person to greet him was Arora
Atlas – she of the good posture and slithering muscles.

"Cheer up," Arora said kindly, clapping Throt on
the arm. "Worse things happen at sea. If you stand tall,
you feel tall. That's my advice!"

And she strode off, followed by the Bonrock
Gymnastics Team, while Throt crawled behind a rock
and howled like a wounded owl.

The visitors were led to the square where the Queen
was waiting, dressed in her finest outfit, which looked
like a caterpillars' graveyard.

The horns went

**PA-PA-PAAAA PAH!**

"Welcome to Brutalia, you poor, scared little Bonrockians!" The Queen made an attempt at a warm smile. "There's no need to fear us, so long as you've brought me some gifts."

"Of course we have," said the Beast of Bonrock, who was sitting on the solid shoulders of Arora Atlas.

He clapped his little hands, and Bonrockians filed on to the stage with sacks of asparagus and lettuce, bottles of elderflower fizz and cakes made with the finest honey. (Sally had snaffled the tomatoes the moment they arrived at the docks.)

The Queen stared down at the foodstuffs. She'd been hoping for something shinier. "Is that it?"

The Beast of Bonrock laughed. "Of course not. We also bring you this..."

On a cushion of squishiest velvet, he presented a crown – a headband with turrets, all made of gold, and each one embedded with a dazzling opal.

"Made by our children during metalwork class. The gemstones were mined just for you."

"Oh!" The Queen's eyes lit up. "It's – it's—"

"It's fit for a Queen who once thought she was a god and lives with a sad waft of disappointment," the Beast added, with a slight smile.

"Yes, yes! How did you know?"

"We did our homework," the Beast said. "And we read Mort the Meek's Monstrous Quest." (Book Two, you rats!)

The Queen nestled the crown atop her head. "Now let us show you round our fabulous island. There's lots to see, and we have regular shows throughout the day."

"Wonderful," Beast said, kicking a rat off his shoe. "We want to see how you live, and learn your customs so that we may understand each other better."

The visitors were paired with Brutalians, who were to act as guides. Mort and Weed stood aside and watched their fellow citizens drag the poor guests around (some by the hands, others by the hair), but the two faces they were looking for were nowhere to be seen.

"Don't tell me they stayed behind," Weed moaned. "I really wanted to see them."

"Me too. They must be here. All of this is because

of them. Because of us. It started with the four of us at Crashbang Cove... That's it! Come on!"

They ran through the stinking side streets and boggy backstreets of Brutalia, all the way to Crashbang, where they had first spotted the *Pax Navi* on the rollicking wash.

There, by the boulder, were two figures.

"Genia! Vita!" Weed cried. "Why are you here?"

"Why are YOU here?" Vita laughed.

"Looking for you!"

"And we were looking for you. Bonrock and Brutalia are friends. Isn't this incredible!"

"You have no idea how incredible it is," Mort said.

"Well, we do actually because we always do our homework," Genia said. "For generations, Brutalia has been known as the loneliest island on Earth. Until now."

"It's worked out brilliantly," said Weed. "Everyone's happy."

"Not quite everyone. Look."

Mort pointed along the cliff where the figure of Throt Gutsem stood, staring out to sea, all forlorn like a hungry tiger who's been given quiche.

"What's the matter with him?" Vita asked.

"He didn't get his battle," Mort said. "His pride turned sour, and now it's turned sad."

"What a shame," Genia said. "But sometimes there have to be losers. It's just a fact."

"That's a very black-and-white way of looking at things," Mort said, and Genia gave a little huff.

Vita said. "In war, *everyone* loses, don't they?"

They looked at each other meaningfully, and ravens drew near, hoping they no longer needed their eyeballs.

"Would you like us to take you on a tour of the island?" Weed asked, knocking a raven away.

"Actually, we'd like to know more about YOU," Genia said. "Why don't you introduce us to your families?"

Mort and Weed looked at each other nervously.

"We can see you're worried," Vita said. "But you are you, and we like you as you are. Nothing will change that."

Genia nodded sincerely. "And nothing you show us can be any stranger than anything we've already seen."

"You don't know what you don't know," Weed said, with a grin. "Like, did you know my dad will try to make you eat one of his slug-paste doughnuts?"

"And that my mum will ask you to throw cutlery at the neighbours?" Mort sighed.

"And we can always say NO," Genia said. "It's a simple word, but surprisingly effective."

## PA-PA-PA-PAAAAAAA-PA!

It looked as if the home visits would have to wait. The first display was about to begin.

Vita opened up a leaflet. "We were given this on arrival. It's an itinerary of events. And it says the first one is... Oh, that's strange."

Mort stood at one end of the stage, and the Queen stood at the other. Between them, the floor had been divided into squares, and in a few of those squares were things that could cause a lot of damage – manky-breath tigers, Grot Bears and guards holding spears.

Mort's punishment was not only going to be painful, it was also going to be witnessed by the whole of Brutalia and the diplomatic envoy from Bonrock, who, for the first time, did look scared.

Marcus Sucram stepped forward. "Mort Canal, you must cross the courtyard and beg the Queen's forgiveness. That's it. Off you go."

Mort looked down at the faces looking up. The Brutalians were quite excited. The Bonrockians were quite horrified. Vita and Genia clung to each other like limpets in a storm. Weed's chocolatey eyes grew wider than a jumbo slug-paste doughnut, and his expression was saying, *I wish this wasn't happening.*

*I wish.*

Mort looked back with a face that said, *HANG ON!*

"Hang on. I have a wish!" he shouted. "I'd like to claim it."

"Absolutely not," spat the Queen. "Now get on with it."

"No."

It was a word he'd learned from Genia. A good word

when used to stand up to bullies.

"I have a right to claim my wish."

"I never gave you one," the Queen said. "You can't prove it."

"But I can." Scribe Pockle stepped forward with his un-scrolled scroll. "It says right here that one wish is owed to Mort Canal."

"UNFAIR! ARGH!"

The Queen had a good old a toddler tantrum in front of the guests. Her scream – which was so shrill it could pierce the eyebrows and uvulas of everyone in a three-mile radius – ricocheted down the side streets and backstreets, causing every adult, child and rat to freeze in their tracks. The Grot Bears and manky-breath tigers recoiled, as if they'd eaten bad clams. And then there was silence.

The Queen, who had made a fool of herself, sobbed into her caterpillary sleeves, and Mort turned to the audience. Weed was grinning and Vita and Genia were looking relieved, as if they'd finally gone to the loo after a long journey. But it was someone else that caught Mort's eye. A sad figure at the back, who was barely recognizable. Perhaps, even in the depths of the direst situation, everyone could be a *winner*.

"So, Mort Canal, do we assume that you are spending your wish on cancelling your punishment?" asked Scribe Pockle.

"No. I wish to continue."

There was a collective gasp from the audience.

The scribe cupped his ear. "Sorry, did you just say no?"

"Yes, I said NO," Mort clarified. "I would like to continue the punishment, but my wish is that I am helped by **THROT GUTSEM**. He is skilled in the strategies of battle, and I just know that he'll get me safely across the Courtyard of Doom. He will stake his pride on it. Throt Gutsem, will you help me with your superior skills of strategy and cunning? If you win, I win. If I win, you win. What do you say?"

At the sound of his name, Throt looked up. At the words **superior skills of strategy and cunning**, he straightened. And he kept straightening until he was full height.

"Nice posture," noted Arora Atlas.

And so the punishment commenced – and what a show it was. Roaring bears and snappy tigers, guards with prodding sticks.

While Mort threw himself physically into the task, Throt threw his brain into the strategy. He paced the sidelines and eyed the positions of Mort and of the aggressors, and he stroked his chin. It sharpened his concentration and whetted his will to win. He advised Mort to hop left, right, backwards and forwards, while bears stumbled into each other, and guards suddenly found themselves next to tigers, and fights broke out among the very nasty elements that had been put there to get Mort.

Every time Mort cleared another space and got away from the claws of a bear or the hot, manky breath of a tiger, the crowd would roar Throt's name, and his Battle-Chief face would brighten, and his steely eyes would come alive. Because Mort was just a prawn; it was Throt who was the king crustacean. It was Throt who was winning the fight – him and his tactical brain.

"One leap to the left, then forward and you're home and dry, boy!" Throt Gutsem shouted.

Mort leaped. Left. A Grot Bear moved towards him on his right, and a tiger came up from behind. But it was too late. Mort jumped forward and bowed low before the Queen.

"I have come to beg your forgiveness," he said.

"Yeah, whatever."

Before the Queen could throw another tantrum, Beast leaped on to the stage.

"I'm impressed. This is a very clever game!" he shouted, throwing celebration sapphires, which was much better than the usual celebration carrots, and everyone cheered.

Mort turned to look at Throt, who was as red as a ruby – but not with rage. It was passion and pride that had returned all at once. No longer a carbuncle but a conqueror.

# CHAPTER EIGHTEEN
# EVERYONE'S A WINNER

*"Do they live happily ever after?"*

*"I doubt it."*

*"Why are you so pessimistic, Ratto?"*

*"To avoid disappointment."*

Mort and his friends sat at the docks, watching the sun dangle above the horizon. They pushed shells, stones and whatever else they could find round an old board that they'd divided into squares and painted with two of the very few colours available on Brutalia.

Genia was scribbling in a notebook. "So let's go through the rules again. When a piece lands on an occupied square, it gobbles up the piece already there?"

"And these prawns can only go forward, up or diagonally, one square at a time. Agreed?" Vita looked for approval. "Great."

"And the fish hooks can only move diagonally," Mort confirmed.

Genia repositioned a horseshoe-crab shell. "And this one can do two spaces forward and one diagonally upwards in one move."

For a moment, no one said a word.

"Why?" Weed snorted. "That's so ... random! No one will ever remember that."

Mort shook his head very slightly as a warning, and Vita bit her lip – nobody ever crossed Genia and her brilliant brain. Weed blushed deep purple as the silence gaped like the elasticated waist band of a hippo's pyjamas.

But Genia burst out laughing. Not the sweet tinkling laugh of previous chapters, but a full throaty one full of hiccups and snorts.

Raaa-ha-ha-ha!

"*I have NEVER heard her laugh like that,*" Vita whispered.

"You're totally right!" Genia hooted. "It makes no sense. It's a stupid move!"

"No, it's not! It's not!" Weed protested.

"Yes, it is! It is! What was I thinking?"

Mort grinned. "Perhaps you weren't thinking at all for once, and you enjoyed it. I say the move stays in so we can remember the time Genia didn't think. Hands up who agrees."

Four hands shot in the air.

"That's it, then," Vita said. "We've invented a new game."

"I've written down the rules," Genia said. "Now we just need a bag to keep everything together."

"There's the box that the picnic's in," Vita said.

"Why don't we eat the food and then put the game in the empty chest?"

"Perfect," Mort said. "We'll present it to Throt Gutsem. A game of strategy to keep his brain sharp. He can declare war every day and still keep the peace."

They spread out a blanket and emptied the large picnic box, containing delicious tomatoes and cheese. Weed had brought bread, which they broke and shared round.

"I love picnics," Vita said.

"Sounds a bit violent, doesn't it – picnic?" Mort said.

"How about peace-nic, then?" Weed suggested. "A meal to join people together."

"A feast for friendship," Genia said, and she smiled at Weed who went a bit wobbly.

"Breaking bread to prevent a war," Mort said. "Peace-nic. It's perfect."

***FWAAAAAAAAARP!***

"Oh no, that's the boat. It's leaving for Bonrock," said Genia. "We'd better hurry."

"We'll wave you off," said Weed, with moist eyes. "Will we ever see you again?"

"Of course you will," Genia said. "You're welcome any time. Don't be a stranger."

Mort smiled. **Don't be a stranger**.

They gave each other big hugs that they'd remember for ever, and the girls boarded the ship. They leaned over the side and waved down at the boys as the foghorns blew again, and for a moment it looked like it might be one of those black-and-white romantic films your granny used to watch. Only nothing is black and white. Nothing. Apart from penguins and chessboards. But chess hadn't been invented yet.

"If you come and visit, don't forget to bring the chest!" Vita cried.

"We'll play the game again and again until we're experts!" said Genia.

"Somehow I think Throt will be the all-time greatest Chest Master. Do you think—"

*FWAAAAAAAAARP!*

*swish, splish, snappy-snap*

*(that's the sound of a boat slowly moving away from the docks while being chased by sharks)*

"I said, do you think ... if Throt really likes it, he

might give up wanting to go to war? Perhaps he'd even consider becoming a pacifist!"

"A what?" Vita shouted over the naval noises and inconvenient distance.

"A pacifist!" Mort yelled.

"Oh, I though your said pass a fist! Wait, that's it!"

"What?"

"Your leaflets! It was a mixing up of homophones!"

Mort and Weed slowly turned to each other, realization dawning like a large orange in a small fruit bowl. Of course! Some people couldn't read, so the message had spread by word of mouth:

## "Pass-a-fist revolution! NOW!"

"War starts with misunderstanding," Mort said. "Fear and misunderstanding."

"Next time we need to word it a bit better."

"Come to think of it, revolution also sounds a bit like an uprising or a revolt, which is bound to make people rise up and be revolting."

"How about we just talk to people instead?" Weed suggested.

"Good idea, Weed. We could have a peace-nic,"

Mort said. "Invite everyone to come and eat and break bread and—"

"Swap recipes."

"Yes, yes. We could swap recipes."

"Practise telling jokes."

"Yes, that too."

"Teach more people to read."

"Now that is a really good idea, Weed, especially if we could find someone willing to teach a bunch of troublesome kids," Mort said. "But I was thinking more of spreading the word of peace. That's it! To avoid confusion, we'll call ourselves peace-nickers."

"Sounds a bit like underwear, Mort. Peaceniks might be better."

"You're right. Oh, look, it's Sally!"

Sally McRoot was heading for the cliffs with a white bird tucked under her arm.

"What are you doing?" Weed called.

"Sending a pigeon to them Bonrockers with a message to bring more tomatoes."

"Why have you painted your pigeon white?"

"So the writing will stand out." She turned the bird

round so the boys could see it.

# Send more tormadus for me soop

"We do live in a totally bonkers place, don't we, Mort?" Weed sighed happily.

"Oh yeah. This island is as mad as a disco in a kipper factory, but I think we just made it kinder."

"Kinda what?"

As a white bird soared to a not-so-strange land with a message of ~~peace~~ **tomatoes** spelled wrongly, the beautiful, ugly sounds of a punk rock song called 'Death to Death' drifted to them on the breeze.

"A kinda nice place to live, Weed. A kinder, nicer place to live."

# THE END

"Well, I suppose that's the end," Mort said. "A happy ending for everyone, wouldn't you say, Weed?"

**"MORT CANAL! I WANT A WORD WITH YOU!"**

(You didn't really think the writer would leave a highly frustrated giant-thumbed thug on the loose, did you?)

The boys turned to see the highly frustrated giant-thumbed thug lumbering towards them.

"Lance Pollip," Weed gulped. "And this time we really do have nowhere to go – we're trapped. It's a choice between death by salty swordfish or death by powerful thumbs."

Mort looked about desperately. Weed was right. Behind them, the rocky harbour was leaping with man-eating beasts, and in front of them...

"Why is he so intent on killing us?"

It was a question they'd have to ask the man himself. Because suddenly he was right there.

"What do you want from us?" Mort yelled. "*What*? What have we ever done to you?"

Lance bent over the boys, like a bear about to catch

salmon. But he didn't try to eat them. Instead, he whispered as sweet and low and gravelly as a river bed, *"I'd like to join the pacifist revolution. Where do I sign up?"*

Mort blinked rapidly, like a clam in a sandstorm. "Pardon?"

"That's what I've been trying to talk to you about, but you kept running away. I saw your leaflets, and I want to be a pacifist, please."

"But you squeeze people to death!" Weed squeaked.

"Not on purpose. I need to find something else I'm good at, that's all..."

Three things happened to Mort simultaneously:

I.   A realization dawned – their reaction had been no better than the Queen's or Tickety-Boo's. But instead of fight they had chosen flight.

2.   Another realization dawned – Lance could read!

3.   He was hit with an idea that was more brilliant than the diamonds that would one

day be discovered in Brutalia's lumps of brown stuff.

"Lance Pollip, how do you fancy being a literacy teacher? Your skills are needed here."

"And the kids won't misbehave – not with your reputation," Weed added.

"Precisely, Weed, just what I was thinking. What do you say, Lance?"

The former boil doctor of Brutalia nodded, and a grin spread across his face like a sunrise over the Serengeti. "All right."

"Oh, and Lance?"

"Yeah?"

"Welcome to the Pacifist Society of Brutalia."

# THE HAPPY ENDING

(you can take off your rat costume now)

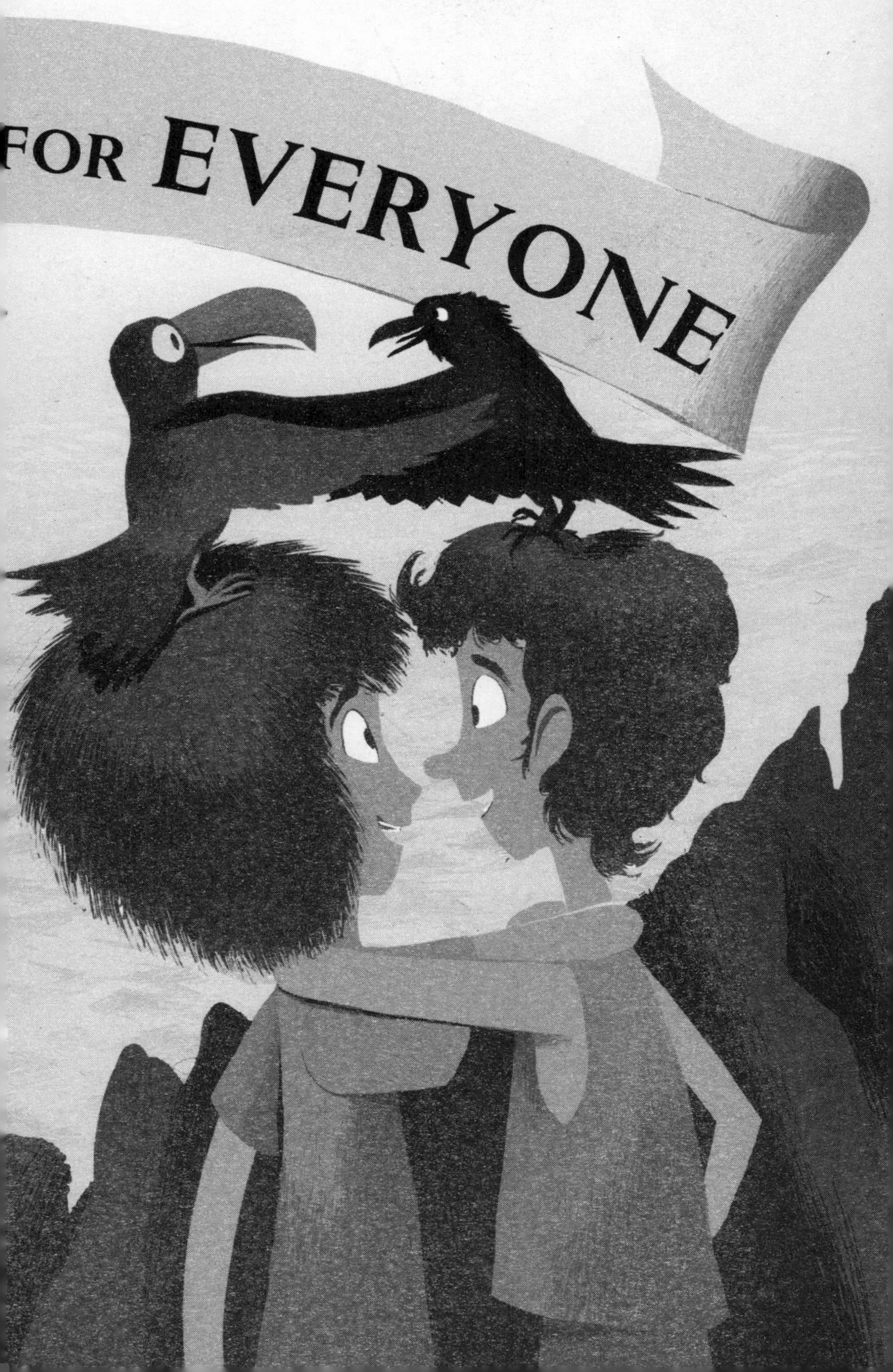
FOR EVERYONE

# ACKNOWLEDGEMENTS

Writing Mort the Meek has been one of life's real joys, and I couldn't have done it without the support of many people. So, thank you to my lovely agent, Alice Williams who was the first to laugh (in a good way); to my amazing family and friends; and to everyone in the brilliant writing community. There's a whole worldwide web of wonderful people out there, but I will mention fellow middle-grade writers, Gareth P Jones, Sinead O'Hart, Tom Easton, Mimi Thebo, Jo Nadin, Lou Abercrombie, Fleur Hitchcock, Gabriel Dylan and Darren Simpson. Thanks also to all the children's book bloggers that read and review, helping to spread the word, including Liam James at BookWormHole, KC at Casey's Pages, Jo Clarke, Sadie at Raising Little Readers, Claire at Home.Read.Play, Amy at GoldenBooksGirl and Sue at Through the Bookshelf.

I owe huge gratitude to the whole team at Little Tiger and of course to George Ermos, whose illustrations

have been a wickedly perfect pairing with the Mort
books, bringing the characters to life and providing
those stunning, eye-popping covers. Thanks also to
Glen McCready for his fantastically fruity narration of
the Mort audiobooks.

And finally, thank you thank you thank you ad
infinitum to Mattie Whitehead, my editor, who picked
up my crazy idea of a pacifist fighting for peace and gave
Mort a fighting chance. This has been the wildest ride
and the most fun I've had with words.

Peace, out.

Rachel Delahaye was born in Australia but
has lived in the UK since she was six years old.
She studied linguistics and worked as a magazine
writer and editor before becoming a children's author.
Rachel loves reading, cooking and wandering about
in woodlands. Somewhere in between all that she
writes. She especially enjoys writing comedy and says,
profoundly: Life without comedy is like cereal
without milk – dry and hard to swallow.

Rachel has two lively children and a dog called Rocket,
and lives in the beautiful city of Bath.

George Ermos is an illustrator, maker and avid reader from England. He works digitally and enjoys illustrating all things curious and mysterious.